FACING

THE STARS

FACING
THE STARS

REBECCA ROSSI

Serenity Press books may be ordered through booksellers or by contacting:

Serenity Press
www.serenitypress.org
serenitypress@hotmail.com

ISBN: 978-0-9945265-6-4 (sc)
ISBN: 978-0-9945265-7-1 (e)

Printed in Australia

"It is the stars…the stars above us,
govern our conditions…"
William Shakespeare

DEDICATION

To my mother and best friend.
Thank you for believing in me.
Where you lead, I will follow…

ACKNOWLEDGEMENTS

Wow! What a whirlwind! Seeing Astrology Pond in published form gave me the drive to continue the series. After two years of brainstorming, writing and rewriting, Facing the Stars is finally here! Originally, I was only going to make this a two book series but somewhere along the way, I realised there was so much more to this story that needed to be told and for this reason, it will be expanded into a trilogy.

I really want to thank my family and friends for supporting me during this time and believing in the story. I also want to give a big thank you to my husband-to-be Francis. You have listened to me natter on about plotlines, character development and the stars for three years now and I'm so grateful for your love and support each and every day.

Lastly, I would like to thank anybody and everybody that picks up this book. Without the readers, it would remain an untold story so I am forever grateful to you all for making it come alive.

Rebecca xx

PROLOGUE

In the Cavern of Red, an angry ram paces the fiery stone floors.

In the Cavern of Green, a cheeky bull swishes its tail in amusement.

In the Cavern of Yellow, two identical brothers spar, their grunts echoing off the cave walls.

In the Cavern of White, an anxious crab clicks its pincers, anticipating what's to come.

In the Cavern of Gold, a lion roars with contempt.

In the Cavern of Grey, a swirling mist surrounds a beautiful maiden who smirks at her own reflection in a crystal mirror.

In the Cavern of Blue, a woman is weighed down by injustice.

In the Cavern of Maroon, venom drips down a scorpion tail.

In the Cavern of Purple, an alluring centaur notches an arrow to his bow.

In the Cavern of Black, a wise old goat sits patiently on his rock.

In the Cavern of Aqua, a man overlooks the sea from his window.

In the Cavern of Sea Foam, seductive sisters flick their tails and giggle with excitement.

They wait, they watch, they are ready…

TABLE OF CONTENTS

PART I

THE MISSION

Chapter 1

Where in the World?

Danni's head was throbbing, her neck and shoulders tense and sore. It was so cold she noticed her fingernails had turned a dark blue. If Danni knew one thing in this world, it was that she had no idea where she was…

Sitting up, she tried to get her bearings but her vision from the drop was blurry. To her left was a mop of red hair that belonged to either Parry or Hannah and there appeared to be bodies littered all over the room. She was so disoriented, she didn't race to check if they were dead or alive. Instead, she lay back down to rest her head. The pounding in her ears had to stop eventually. Where was she again? Suddenly, the strong smell of leather forced reality to hit her hard.

Garth! Was her nightmare real? Did she really just lose one of her closest friends and the Astro A Team before jumping into the pond at Bouquet Reserve? Maybe someone had slipped something in her dinner because she was pretty certain a pond was just a pond, not a portal to an alternate universe!

Jumping to her feet, she raced over and shook the unidentified red mop. The girl stirred and rolled over, revealing two blue eyes the size of saucers. Immediately, they filled with tears and the girl sat up, shivering and grasping at Danni like a frightened cat.

'Hannah! It's okay, it's me!' Danni rubbed the scared girl's shoulders.

Hannah flung her arms around Danni and sobbed. Danni felt something sticky against her cheek. She drew her friend back to find a gash on Hannah's forehead dripping like a broken tap.

'This looks pretty nasty.' Danni grabbed Hannah's hand. 'Let's go see if someone can patch it up.'

'How can you be so calm, Danni?' Hannah continued to cry. 'Where are we? Where is Drew and…?'

She stopped short and Danni saw her notice the slumped over figures occupying what appeared to be a large cavern with an incredibly high ceiling.

With a scream of terror, Hannah raced to a crumpled over Drew.

'Snuggly bear! It's me…Hanny!' She shook him so hard Danni felt dizzy.

Drew gave a massive groan and rolled over, squinting up at his girlfriend's concerned face.

'Where the hell am I?' he muttered.

Hannah squeezed him until he let out a loud cough. Danni knelt next to both of them, putting her hand on Drew's.

'We are exactly where Garth said he was taking us…Bastion…Home of the Stars.'

'Right,' Drew croaked. 'And I am Salvador Dali…what odd paintings you turned out to be.'

Danni stood up and straightened her clothes. They were full of dirt marks, scrapes and her fashionable worn out jeans were now actually worn out.

'I know it sounds ridiculous but I'm pretty sure we didn't all dream the same dream. We jumped into the pond at Bouquet Reserve, blacked out and woke up here…wherever that is?'

Hannah snuggled into Drew who was now wincing in pain. It didn't look like he had suffered major injuries but he was evidently winded.

'Danni, we need to go home.' Hannah pressed her sleeve against the cut in her forehead. 'Drew and I are badly hurt. If the pond was a portal, there must be a way to get back.'

The three of them scanned the large cavern. The only things that stood out were the other bodies. There didn't seem to be any lights, exits, entrances, flashing neon signs saying "portal home" or any indication they were even on Earth.

'How can this be it?' Drew wondered aloud.

Danni pulled both Hannah and Drew to their feet and began walking over to the rest of her group.

'Look, let's at least find Garth; he is sure to have all the answers.'

'Why didn't you ever tell us about him, Dan?'

Danni looked back at one of her best friends. Perhaps her only best friend now that Reilly hated her.

'You already thought I was weird. How would you have reacted if I told you Morpheus from *The Matrix* was hanging around my bedroom?'

Drew shrugged. 'I probably would've had you committed but you still should've told me.'

'My point exactly! Can you please wake up Reilly? I'm pretty sure she never wants to speak to me again.'

She could tell Drew was about to protest and promise false hope so she silenced him with a look and pointed to a figure near the far east of the cavern. Danni wanted nothing more in that moment than to run over to the girl with tangled black hair on the stone floor and hug her the way she did the night of the Astrological Dance but it wouldn't be well received.

Watching Drew and Hannah traipse over to Reilly, she suddenly felt incredibly lonely. The three of them would always have each other to lean on but who would Danni have?

Feeling a tap on her shoulder, she spun around to see Parry looking so dishevelled it took her a moment to register who it really was.

Without saying anything, Danni threw herself into Parry's arms, remembering the love and loyalty he had shown her before they had jumped. Parry squeezed Danni back. They hugged for a few seconds before breaking apart and laughing awkwardly.

'I'm so glad you don't hate me,' Danni smiled.

'I could never hate you, Dan.' Parry shook her head furiously. 'What I do hate is being stuck in some weird-ass cave without fresh clothes and a hair straightener!'

Danni chuckled. She had grown fond of Parry's vanity.

'So *you* know this isn't a dream, right?'

'How could it be? I've never seen *this* much detail in my dreams!'

Parry swung her head left and right, scanning the bodies and looking anxious.

'I'm sure he's here somewhere and just fine,' Danni reassured her.

The beautiful girl nodded and brought a fingernail to her teeth to gnaw on before stopping and looking at it in disgust.

'I know, it's just that he was going to leave that night, Dan, and we somehow convinced him to stay. If he is hurt in any way, it will be our fault. Maybe we should have let him leave and then he wouldn't have wound up here with us.'

'How do you think I feel? If it wasn't for me even starting the Astro A Team we wouldn't be in this mess and my best friend would still love me.'

Parry gave a shrug that wasn't entirely unfeeling.

'Life is meant to be lived, Dan. Can we go find Graham now?'

Danni frowned. 'Let's find Graham and get some answers!'

Chapter 2

A New Universe

Danni and Parry walked to the centre of the cavern where they saw more and more members waking and looking around in confusion. Brodie was massaging her leg that sported a purple bruise so big Danni screwed up her face in discomfort. Hunter had his head in his hands, with Ambrite's loving arm around him. Danni frantically searched the wide space to make sure Reilly wasn't hurt. Her eyes met Slade who didn't appear injured just incredibly dusty. She hated how good he looked even after travelling by portal. He gazed at her sadly and moved towards her but she quickly turned and walked to Parry who was kissing Graham on both cheeks and sobbing.

'Darling, it's quite all right! I chose to stay didn't I?' Graham stroked the Virgo's red locks.

'Wha...what if we can't le...leave?' Parry shook and showered her face with tears.

'Then we die together!' Graham bellowed. 'We give our beautiful corpses to the dust and stars…immortalised in beauty for all eternity…'

'Dramatic much?' A familiar, sarcastic voice muttered behind Danni.

She turned and saw Ronan, slightly out of sorts but still his old Capricorn self.

Like Parry, she remembered his support before they jumped and felt her eyes well up.

'You know, it's funny…when I first met you, I honestly thought you were rude, sexist and a massive headache but you've turned out to be one of my closest friends and I can't let you go.'

Ronan laughed and put his hands on her shoulders. They met each other's gaze and Danni suddenly felt self-conscious and puffy.

'Dan, I'm a logical guy as you know and what you did, whilst a bit reckless, was not malicious. I saw how sorry you were and how desperately you wanted Reilly's forgiveness. You're a good person and no matter what happens, I'll never forget what you did for me and my family.'

Danni nodded and brushed the wetness from her cheeks. She looked up and saw Drew, Hannah and Reilly talking in a corner. Her former best friend appeared stable but angry. She wondered whether it would be wise to try and talk to her again.

Ronan suddenly cleared his throat, making Danni jump.

'So...do you think you'll try and give things with Slade a go now that they're out in the open?'

Danni noticed Ronan wasn't meeting her gaze anymore. She began to reply, 'Err...well to be honest...'

'WHERE THE HELL ARE WE AND WHERE IS THAT GOTH FREAK MAN?'

The pitch and intensity of Charlotte's voice was enough to cave in the entire...cave! Danni huffed. In all the fuss and worry, she had completely forgotten about the additional passenger that had caused all the drama in the first place.

Charlotte was a sight to see indeed. Wet, stringy hair with flecks of mud hung from her scalp. Her strappy dress was torn and ripped at the end. A giant welt marked the side of her chin and some broken fingernails hung loosely from her no-longer manicured hands. Crawford's curly hair contained the same mud and disarray and his shirt was wet in the patches Charlotte would've gripped onto. Danni still had no idea what he saw in that spoiled brat.

At the sound of Charlotte's cries, the entire group began to form a circle in the centre and looked to Danni to lead. Hesitant, she began to trudge forward, ignoring death glares from Charlotte, Ambrite and a forced disinterested look from Reilly. She visualised the beautiful, calm pond back in Bouquet Reserve and took a deep breath.

'So…obviously we are all sore, confused and anxious. We have no idea where we are and I don't know about you guys but I'm starting to think Garth was taking us all for a ride…literally!'

'We shouldn't have trusted him!' Hannah called out.

Danni nodded. 'Probably not but we are here now and together we have to figure out a way to get home. I highly doubt we are in an alternate universe called Bastion which is home to our astrological counterparts…or whatever that crackpot was on about.'

'Crackpot, hey? Well remind me never to take you on a whirlwind adventure again!'

Everybody turned to see Garth leaning against the wall looking immaculate in a black tuxedo and satin top hat.

'Sorry! I had to change before the induction!'

Everybody stared with open mouths until Parry stamped her foot, creating echoes.

'This whole time we have been sick with anxiety! Some of us are hurt. Just look at Hannah's forehead! My hair has not been this frizzy since I was eight years old and here you strut along in a penguin suit which by the way does not suit the décor of this cave at all! Why are you wearing it and tell us where the exit is!'

Garth stared at Parry for a good minute before bursting into laughter. He leaned his weight against the side wall to keep from toppling over.

'My sides...oh my gosh...please stop...it's too much...you're all so adorable.'

'Listen here, Bond! You better give us some answers or we'll wipe the floor with you!' Ambrite snarled.

The Taurean's angry outburst set Garth off again and he sank into a heap emitting peal after peal of laughter.

Danni looked over at Charlotte who was the dirtiest of the lot and grinned.

'Charlotte, I think you should go over and give our suited up friend a nice big bear hug.'

For the first time since they had met Charlotte grinned back and began walking over to Garth, arms outstretched.

'Okay, okay!' Garth yelled and hopped backwards, all signs of laughter gone. 'This suit is *Gucci* and I don't get the chance to shop on Earth very often!'

Brodie hobbled over and stood next to her brother. 'Earth? So we aren't even on the planet anymore?'

Garth groaned dramatically and looked toward the ceiling in frustration.

'Did you not all listen when I said we were going to an alternate universe called Bastion to save the stars and meet with your astrological counterparts? Was I speaking

Bulgarian? This is where we are and the reason for my chuckle fest is because this cave is literally a speck in comparison to how big Bastion really is.'

Hunter, who looked ready to tackle Garth, balled his hands into fists.

'Then where are the exits, doors, windows or some sign that life exists outside of this damn cave?'

Garth rolled his eyes. 'The lights are currently off. When the lights turn on, Aries, you will see that this cave is a stony palace!'

'You do realise that Bastion isn't a place we visit on the summer holidays,' Reilly retorted. 'We have never been here before so how were we supposed to know a bloody light switch makes this place come alive?'

Danni let out a snort which quickly turned into a cough when she saw Reilly glare in her direction.

'Why do Fire Signs have to be the most difficult? First the Aries, then the Sagittarius giving me sass. Do you want to give me lip too, boy?'

Garth raised a challenging eye at Crawford.

Crawford put his hands up in surrender and turned to Drew who shrugged.

Reilly took a feisty step forward. 'We give you lip because we were having the night from hell and then you showed up and took us to Lucifer's lair itself! We want answers and we want them now!'

Garth walked over to Danni and rested his arm on her shoulder.

'Help me out here, buddy. Tell your friends to behave.'

Danni raised her eyebrows and shook his arm off. 'My friends will behave when you give them answers, medical treatment, some clean clothes, food and a hot shower.'

The entire group including Reilly whooped in agreement.

'All right my little munchkins,' Garth crooned. 'I do need you all in good shape if you're going to save the universe! Let me ask the boss to turn on the lights.'

'The boss? Aren't you the boss?' Slade frowned.

'Pfft! Amateurs! The lot of you,' Garth groaned.

'I really think you should stop expecting us to know everything.' Hannah spoke politely.

'Wait,' Danni interjected. 'Is your boss that Asterion guy you said you were the advisor for?'

Garth looked utterly offended. 'That Asterion guy? Let me break it down for you, Gem. I am the Chief Advisor to Asterion, Keeper of the Stars and Guardian of Bastion.'

'Whatever that means,' Ambrite muttered.

'It means everything, you wild child!' Garth said. 'Asterion has personally selected you twelve to save the entire universe and restore order to the stars above. You'd think you'd be a little more grateful.'

Danni noticed the group getting angrier and she herself felt frustrated at Garth's proficiency for being so vague. She turned to Garth and softened her tone.

'Why us, Garth? There are billions of people on Earth and you picked us.'

Garth appeared thoughtful. 'Because nobody else on this planet loves astrology the way you do, Danni.'

The answer was so simple yet powerful. It made Danni's heart swell with pride.

'Nobody in this universe has ever expressed such a deep love and devotion for the stars. Sure, there are astrologers and it's very popular in your western culture but you actually wanted to learn the secrets *behind* them. We have been searching for somebody with your level of commitment for a long time and once I found you, I just had to help "guide" you to find the rest of your team.'

The group all shifted their gaze to Danni. She felt uncomfortably on display.

'I knew you were helping me with my dreams. If it wasn't for you, I wouldn't have met such amazing people and had the time of my life so I am grateful. Whatever we can do to help "save the universe" we will do.'

'Excellent!' Garth rubbed his hands together. 'Asterion should be here shortly to brief you on your mission. And just a side note, when I say "save the universe" I am being a little dramatic…'

'Hey! I'm not doing anything unless I save mankind and continue looking macho for Hannah.' Drew puffed out his chest then winced in pain.

Garth looked at Hannah who was giggling and narrowed his gaze. Instantly, her forehead was no longer bleeding and a thick strip of bandage covered the gash. She let out a squeal of joy.

'Anybody else who has injuries please come forward and I'll put them right.'

Brodie hobbled over along with Drew who was still winded. Hunter produced a dislocated shoulder that turned Danni's stomach. One by one Garth focused on the injuries and they were instantly repaired.

'How do you do that, man?' Drew asked in awe, his voice no longer strained.

'I am Garth, Chief Advisor to…'

'Yeah, yeah we've heard the spiel! Tell us why this mission isn't as urgent as you made it out to be,' Ronan interrupted.

'Rudeness!'

Garth slammed his hand against the wall making everybody jump. A second later he let out a chuckle. Danni was starting to worry that the Chief Advisor was mentally unstable.

'Just kidding! I'll let Asterion explain it properly when he arrives but basically we have brought all of you here to prevent a problem that could end up causing devastation and destruction.'

'So in other words we are here to stop something that may or may not end up happening,' Graham said.

The cave was beginning to darken and before Garth could answer the entire room was thrown into complete blackness.

Suddenly, a giant crack like the sound of a whip being flung rang out, making Danni's ears ache. The cavern was filled with giant arches set against the walls. Each one displayed different coloured lights and at the far end stood the biggest set of purple doors Danni had ever seen. Their solidity and structure screamed "exit" and she had to stop herself from running towards them and escaping.

A massive gold throne had appeared in the centre alongside a slightly smaller silver throne. Garth winked at the group before seating himself beside the larger one.

'Whoa,' she heard Drew whisper.

Turning her gaze in his direction, she saw a giant aquarium against the wall located next to the sea green arch. It was filled with seaweed of all colours, fish of all sizes and an enormous stony castle in the centre. The cave had seemed gigantic beforehand but now it resembled a rainbow amusement park.

'Talk about turning the lights on,' Ambrite breathed.

It didn't take Danni long to register that each coloured arch matched its zodiac sign. It reminded her of the Astrological Dance and how they had all coordinated their outfits accordingly. The yellow one stood out to her, bright and alluring. Danni wanted to walk through and find her Gemini counterparts.

Between every arch and the next, a bed appeared with their names printed overhead. Danni saw twin beds pop up beside the yellow portal and felt her heart sink. Of course…she was going to be sharing with Charlotte. She noticed Charlotte reading both of their names and making a face like she'd just sucked on a lemon. The feeling was mutual.

Danni spun around and saw her group running towards the giant purple doors. She raced after them and stopped when a massive food station popped up, emitting the most delicious smells. She watched Reilly tiptoe over and inhale the buffet spread. The Sagittarian had never been able to resist food!

Her stomach rumbled and for the first time since arriving, she thought of home. Her parents would be asleep by now and time would be moving very slowly. Shaking off her homesickness and hunger she watched Hunter and Ronan attempt to pry the doors open. She could hear Garth chuckling in the background which indicated that their attempts to escape were useless.

The smell of steam and coconut oil diverted Danni's attention. A wooden bathhouse had been set up on the other side of the food station. Parry let out a squeal and ran into the bathhouse without caution. It wasn't long before Danni heard a gush of water and a voice singing pop songs. Charlotte, looking like a filthy mess, grabbed Crawford's hand and smirked at Danni before pulling him into one of the showers. Danni laughed it off. Her feelings for Crawford were long gone and since losing Reilly, the ones for Slade were rapidly disappearing as well. Before she had met both ex-flames, her idea of love was perfect and without flaw. Since meeting them, she realised it was nothing but pain and humiliation. It certainly didn't make her want to try again with anybody else.

Returning her gaze to the thrones, she noticed the larger one was still empty and Garth was occupying the smaller one with a cheeky grin. He stood up and yelled across the cave making everybody stop in their tracks. Even the showers had been turned off and the bathhouse was quiet.

'Five more minutes and Asterion will arrive so please finish washing, eating and if you require fresh clothes they have arrived in your wardrobes next to your beds. Everybody meet back here so you can be briefed on your mission.'

Danni smiled sadly as she watched Reilly grabbing some food to go. She wanted to go over and chide her about her appetite like old times. Instead, she walked over to her bed on the left and opened a tall wardrobe that displayed a full-length mirror on the side door and a rack of clothes hanging up neatly. The mirror reflected her horrified face when she realised every article of clothing was bright yellow. From the sunflower leggings to the deep mustard t-shirts, Danni felt like she belonged on some children's television program. She spun around and noticed Parry's mortified expression at the gloomy grey collection and felt envious at Brodie's range of blue outfits. Drew pulled out a pair of sea-green pants and thrust them at Garth, who was once again in tears from laughter, in disbelief. She hated how much he was enjoying all of this.

'Whhhhhyyyyyyy!' Parry wailed.

Garth stopped for a second and walked over to the pouting Virgo. He pulled a face at her grey pleated skirt which made Parry leap on the bed and bury her face, muffling sobs.

Danni felt such empathy, she sat on the edge of Parry's bed and rubbed her back whilst glaring at Garth.

'Why do we have to dress this way? It was all right when we had the Astrological Dance but there is no need to butcher my idea!'

Garth sniffed at her like she was a talking piece of roadkill.

'You obviously don't know how Bastion works, darling. Outside these doors is the city and everybody is dressed in their own colours so you can identify which sign they are. Not only that, your counterparts will not listen to you if you are wearing any other colour than the one they represent. This is a serious mission and you must dress accordingly. Obviously, some of you are luckier than others in colour but you just have to suck it up and pull it off. Right, princess?'

Garth poked Parry in the side and she lifted her head looking like a wet raccoon. Her pillow was streaked with black mascara. She turned the case over pretending nothing had happened.

'Nobody can pull off an outfit like me! You just watch how I'll rock that grey! Funeral wear has never looked so chic!'

Garth jumped off her bed. 'That's the spirit! Statues will be so jealous!'

Danni rolled her eyes and stood up.

'So if you're wearing a black and white *Gucci* suit, which sign are you?'

Garth looked genuinely pleased to be asked that question.

'Asterion and I have no idea or recollection when I was born. It was hundreds of years ago. As I said, time on Bastion is completely different to Earth and my parents were killed shortly after I was born…'

Danni was surprised to witness a glimpse of humanity from the suave Advisor. He noticed her expression and shook his head.

'Don't feel sorry for me, Danni, I don't even remember them. The point I was trying to make was I have no idea what sign I am and therefore I wear whatever colour I choose. Neat, isn't it? There are about fifty Unsigned in Bastion and we can wear whatever colour we like. Those that are Unsigned are generally pitied so our one consolation is a colourful wardrobe.'

Danni listened in fascination. Suddenly, her lemony wardrobe didn't seem so awful. She liked how all the signs could be identified by their colours and felt a touch of sadness for the Unsigned. Being a Gemini was her life, her true identity. It would be awful not knowing which section of the stars you belonged to.

'What about Asterion?' Drew piped up.

'Asterion always wears gold and white to signify his status in Bastion,' Garth continued. 'He likes to joke around that he is a Leo for this reason but he actually refuses to tell anybody which sign he is. He once told me it was so nobody could have an edge over him but I never understood what that meant…'

'Best keep it that way, Garth,' a gentle voice echoed from around the cave.

The entire Astro A Team including Charlotte and Garth turned to see a faint golden light shimmering around the large throne. A tall gangly man began to appear who looked hundreds of years old. Along with his hair, the man's fluffy white beard hung from his chin reaching his torso. He was draped in a white robe, a shiny golden belt fastened around his tiny waist. His golden sandals clung to his wrinkled feet and his teeth were so white they had to be false. In short, his appearance screamed Keeper of the Stars.

Garth stared in awe as if this was their first encounter before hopping over to the small throne, seating himself and gesturing for the others to follow suit. The group seated themselves around the thrones like schoolchildren waiting for their teacher to tell them a story.

Danni heard Ambrite snigger to Hunter, 'Could've just used the giant purple door.'

'I may look like a decrepit old soul but my hearing is supersonic,' Asterion warned. His eyes narrowed at the Taurean but his mouth held the imprint of a smile.

Ambrite flushed in a manner very unlike her and sat up straighter.

Danni watched as Asterion swept his gaze over the group before him, kindly but firmly assessing them all. He stopped when his eyes met Danni's and she felt a tug at her heart. He nodded gently in her direction and turned his attention to Garth.

'You have done very well in bringing them all here. I don't know what you were so worried about.'

Ronan snorted and Garth went beetroot red which made Danni think of the penguin with a sunburn joke.

'I wasn't worried, My Lord,' Garth spluttered. 'I was merely concerned that these teenagers would get too hung up on dating and parties which flies in the face of our master plan!'

'No need to get flustered, they are all here and eager aren't they?' Asterion consoled.

Charlotte, looking remarkably out of place in yellow flannel pyjamas, let out a dramatic sigh. Danni noticed Asterion looking slightly vexed at her "evil twin".

Crawford went to rub her arm but she shook it off as if he were a mosquito.

'We may be here but we are not eager,' Charlotte pouted. 'I wasn't even part of this stupid group and somehow I got dragged here anyway! Can you at least send me home? As you can see there's already one Gemini so my being here is pointless.'

'That's what I tried to tell you when you asked to join the group in the first place!' Danni retorted.

Garth looked ready to rip Charlotte to shreds but Asterion steadied him with a hand. He turned to the outspoken Gemini with a soft face.

'My dear, when Danni goes to face the Gemini counterparts she will be facing not one but two men. They are by far the most devilish, tricky and untrustworthy opponents of them all and she will need you to communicate with one whilst she converses with the other. If you try to reason with both of them together, they will take advantage of you and you'll leave with a muddled mind. It is two against two and that is how it must be.'

Danni suddenly felt sick to her stomach. Not only was she going to be paired with her nemesis but she was facing the toughest twins in the zodiac.

Sensing her discomfort Garth rushed to her aid. 'Charlotte, Asterion is right. You're going to have to unite with Danni if you two are to be successful on your mission. Don't leave her to face the pair alone. It's girls versus boys so go get 'em!'

Danni met eyes with Charlotte before they both rapidly turned away. Maybe once they entered the Cavern of Yellow they would learn to work together…

Danni's train of thought was interrupted by Hunter's deep voice.

'Okay so Dan now knows her and Charlotte are in for a fight. What about the rest of us?'

Asterion nodded. 'It's time for your briefing. I hope by the end of what I have to stay you don't decide to leave…'

Chapter 3

The Rulers of the Stars

By this time, Asterion had captured everybody's attention and nobody dared move let alone speak.

'Before any of you go charging into the Coloured Caverns, you must understand why you are here and what is expected of you. This mission will ultimately test you mentally although I cannot guarantee you won't be harmed…particularly if you anger your counterpart.'

Danni glanced over at Hannah and wasn't surprised to see her whimpering into Drew's hoodie. She felt for the poor girl. This would either make or break her.

'The counterparts have existed in Bastion for thousands of years and are responsible for their constellations in the night sky,' continued Asterion. 'Their power allows the stars to shine and guide astronomers as well as various spacecraft that orbit our galaxy. Without the help of the counterparts, your planet Earth would be plunged into disaster. For one, the sudden absence of twelve very well-known constellations would scare mankind and cause them to question their own existence. For two, our planet would begin to wear away to nothing. The counterparts themselves use their starlight to fuel Bastion and keep it running. I know you Earthlings use electricity but we function purely on starlight and our constant supply comes straight from this cave…'

Graham let out an 'ah-ha'. Garth threw daggers in his direction but Asterion gestured for the Scorpio to speak.

'I think I see now why Garth mentioned that this problem could potentially cause devastation and destruction. Are the counterparts no longer willing to supply starlight to Bastion and their constellations?'

Asterion looked very grave and Garth slumped in his smaller throne.

'Yes…well some are making threats and no amount of discussion and begging will make them see sense. They are much much older than myself and incredibly stubborn. As soon as they began to make these threats, Garth and I knew we had to seek "outside help". Garth used his abilities to search for a person who loved astrology so much they would be willing to drop it all and travel here to save us.'

Danni remembered the night Garth had appeared in her window wearing a dragon necklace. She noticed it now, hanging around his neck as he lounged on his throne and wondered what other powers it possessed.

'Once I found you, Danni, it wasn't too difficult to help you round up the rest of the Astro A Team,' Garth winked.

'What about me?' Charlotte interrupted. 'I was never part of the Astro A Team and if I hadn't shown up that night then Danni would've had to face the counterparts by herself.'

'One thing you must learn, my dear Charlotte is that there is no such thing as coincidence,' Garth chuckled. 'When I said you were both sisters in this universe, I meant it. You must be sisters if you are to face your counterpart brothers.'

'So you purposely led her to the group and ruined my life?' Danni narrowed her eyes.

Charlotte jumped up but Crawford pulled her down, shaking his head. Asterion looked amused and Danni shuffled to the opposite side near Garth's feet.

'Danni, you must learn to make peace with Charlotte or this plan will not work.'

Danni felt torn and angry. She wanted to blame Charlotte for what had happened between her and Reilly. She wanted to hate her for stealing Crawford and trying to turn her friends against her. She wanted to do this alone because Charlotte didn't deserve to be involved in such an important mission. She looked up at Reilly and saw her sad face staring back. She had to let go…

'I'll do my best for the sake of the mission,' Danni spoke.

'That is very wise,' Asterion nodded. 'You don't understand how these counterparts work. They will use your feud with Charlotte and ensure you both continue to fight until you forget your mission. Please understand they do not want you here. They all think you are wasting your time and are ready for you. They will do whatever is necessary to drive you crazy until you are begging to return home.'

Drew's hand shot up in the air and Garth pointed at him.

'Okay, I'm just going to ask the million dollar question here…why now? Why make these threats now after thousands of years?'

'Boom!' Garth punched the air.

'Garth, settle down,' Asterion muttered.

Drew looked pleased with himself and laid a big sloppy kiss on Hannah, causing Ambrite to turn up her pierced nose.

'That is indeed a good question, Drew. The reason for their sudden threats stems from a visitor Bastion received not long ago. We have a neighbouring planet named Cassius which predominantly monitors and ensures the smooth flow of meteoroids throughout the

Solar System.   They protect Earth and its surrounding planets by directing the meteoroids in a straight formation. This important job prevents the meteoroids from passing through the Earth's atmosphere and impacting the surface of your planet. Representatives from Cassius meet with myself and Garth every year and keep us updated. Sometimes we travel there and report on what astronomers have learnt from our constellations. We work together to keep our Solar System safe…'

Ronan leaned forward. 'Is this where you say until now?'

'Unfortunately yes. You see Bastion has always been guarded by myself and a Chief Advisor…'

'I'm the best you've ever had, right?' Garth interjected.

'Yes of course.' Asterion rolled his eyes.

Danni couldn't help but grin.

'But on Cassius, new representatives are chosen every two years and serve for those two years only. The latest election only occurred a few months before the Astro A Team was formed and their latest representative Milo ruined everything with a few words.'

'*Milo!*' Garth raged, his hands curled into fists.

'Wow, not a fan of old Milo,' Slade observed.

'What could Milo have possibly said to bring about the utter destruction of the universe?' Reilly scoffed in disbelief.

'Well…when a representative from Cassius is elected, they are allowed the honour of meeting with all of the counterparts and once they have met, they are never allowed inside this cave again. From what he heard prior to his visit, Milo has proven to be quite power hungry and loves being in control. He wasn't good at hiding his jealousy when he saw just how powerful the counterparts were and took it upon himself to impart some unwanted words of wisdom before he left. Now…I don't actually know what was said but he managed to turn all twelve signs of the zodiac against one another and now they are at war. From what I've gathered from the more placid counterparts, he planted the idea that one sign of the zodiac should rule over all of the others much like Earth has presidents, prime ministers, kings and queens. Since that moment, they have not stopped fighting and refuse to back down. Every single one of them believes they should rule and have threatened to stop producing starlight if they are not picked by myself and Garth.'

'So this is where we step in?' Danni looked around at her group. Some looked terrified, others excited and she was certainly a mixture of both.

'Precisely,' Asterion agreed. 'We need each of you to face your counterparts alone and unite them.'

'Why do you think I kept telling you to stay united with your group, Danni?' Garth pressed. 'It was because you couldn't possibly unite the counterparts unless you yourselves stood together as one. You must lead by example.'

'No pressure or anything,' muttered Hunter.

'Just the destruction of our planet and yours, my dear Aries!' Garth retorted.

'Stop scaring them, Garth,' Asterion scolded. 'As I mentioned earlier, you cannot enter the Coloured Caverns without knowing what you are facing. They are all manipulative in their own way and know things about you that only you know yourself. They will use it against you and play on your fears, insecurities and flaws. You have to be mentally strong and see through their traps. Do not take the bait and whatever you do, do not give up.'

'Why are the zodiac so nasty?' Parry piped up. True to her word, she was looking stylish in a cute woollen grey dress and beanie.

Asterion let out his first laugh. It was deep and booming but friendly.

'They aren't nasty, they are just very old. The majority of them are quite kind but this debate over who should rule has brought out the worst in some of them and they do not want a bunch of teenagers from Earth trying to change their minds. It hurts their pride and they are nothing if not proud.'

'Does Milo realise how much crap he's caused?' Ambrite scorned.

'I'm sure he is very pleased with himself,' Garth growled. 'Luckily he is not permitted to serve longer than two years so we won't have to see him here again.'

Hannah raised her hand. 'Do you think there should be one ruler?'

Asterion shook his head. 'No, my dear.' He spoke so gently that even the Cancerian appeared at ease. 'As I'm sure you have learned from your weekly meetings at Bouquet Reserve, there is no one sign more superior than another. They are all unique, all flawed and all special. Each one balances the others and they need to rule together. Please all do your best to convince your counterparts of this lesson.'

'We will.' Danni stood up. 'I knew there was so much more to the stars than just those crappy daily horoscopes you see in the newspapers dictating that a tall, dark stranger will whisk you away to a foreign land.'

Asterion let out another booming laugh. 'I'm sure the counterparts would destroy those newspapers if they ever laid eyes on them.'

'Soooo…are we ever allowed to leave this place and explore the city?' Parry flicked a lock of red hair around her finger with an innocent wide-eyed look.

The group stared attentively at Asterion whilst he tapped the toe of his sandals repeatedly on the stone floor.

'As you are all aware by now, this mission isn't going to be easy. You could very well fail. You could make the counterparts even angrier and bring about the destruction of our universe even faster. This is going to take time and careful but honest communication. I would be very surprised if you walked through that cavern tomorrow and by the end of the day restored peace. It may take several tries and weeks on end…perhaps months…'

'Months?' Ronan scoffed. 'We don't have months, most of us are still in school and my dad and Brandon need me.'

Garth let out a loud huff. 'Ronan, remember that time moves differently here. A few months here could equate to about five days back home. I will be monitoring all of your families and should they start to worry, I will use my abilities to make them think you just left for your meeting the night you left.'

Ronan nodded, still appearing unconvinced. He looked at Danni and shrugged. She felt her heart hop and quickly fixed her gaze on Asterion.

'As I was saying…I'm not sure how long you are all going to be here but if I see you are making progress, you are more than welcome to explore our city. Bastion is a beautiful place filled with colour, as I'm sure Garth told you about our identification system here. We even have what you Earthlings call a "nightclub".'

Graham and Parry let out a giant squeal which sounded like a squeaky door opening in the echoing cave. They immediately began talking over the top of one another about what they would wear and how they would dance all night. Graham stood up and began shaking his booty in burgundy bell bottoms. Parry shimmied around him and slapped his behind before the Scorpio spun her around and ended the routine in a sultry dip.

The group stared in fascination before all of them burst out laughing, including Garth and Asterion who weren't privy to the usual Graham/Parry ways.

Not even slightly without shame, the pair took a bow and sat down. Asterion clapped his hands and shook his head in wonder.

'Perform a couple of those dance moves on your counterparts and you may just win them over! I'm willing to let you explore and enjoy a night at Constellar provided things aren't too dire here. If I can see the tensions are rising we may need to work overtime, doing everything we can to keep them calm.'

'Yes and in the meantime you will be absolutely pampered here with food, showers, comfortable bedding and a fully stocked wardrobe,' Garth added.

Danni couldn't wait for her turn in the showers; she could still smell the coconut oil from Parry's skin.

Hunter stuck his arm awkwardly in the air. 'This may sound like a dumb question…'

'There are no dumb questions, Hunter,' Asterion soothed.

Hunter looked at Ambrite before proceeding. 'What if I want to go with Ambrite into her cavern as support? I know a lot about her life and I'm worried the counterpart will use it against her.'

Asterion frowned.

'Hunter, it is so kind of you to want to support Ambrite and I'm not going to sugar-coat this in any way, shape or form. The counterpart will most likely hit her where it hurts the most but you are absolutely forbidden to enter her cavern. This is something she must do on her own as you must also do on your own. If her counterpart sees you, he will lose his temper and our entire mission could be jeopardised. You will have plenty of time between visits to support one another in the Mission Base as this area is known...and for the record that is an excellent question.'

Ambrite rubbed Hunter's shoulder and reassured him she would be fine. He looked so crestfallen Danni wanted to reach over, hug him and tell him how far he had come from the incredibly angry boy she had met in the waiting room.

It was really starting to become clear that aside from Danni and Charlotte, the rest of the Astro A Team needed to work independently and be mentally prepared for the deep, dark secrets that were undeniably going to surface. Danni's head was starting to throb and her limbs felt stiff from sitting down for so long. She really hoped they were coming to the end of their briefing. Whilst it had been extremely helpful, nothing could truly prepare them for the real thing.

Asterion stood from his throne and gestured for Garth to do the same. They walked over to the Cavern of Red which was Hunter's. Standing at either side with their backs to the entrance, they both held out their hands to the group who had huddled over.

'Astro A Team…and Charlotte,' Garth began. 'We are in awe of your bravery, your wisdom and commitment to the stars. Whether you succeed or not, we are proud of the young adults you've become and are confident in your abilities to unite not only the counterparts but each other. Take care of one another. Tomorrow at dawn, the Coloured Caverns will become active and you will walk through to your destiny. I'm sure you've all thought you won't get sucked in by your counterparts. I'm telling you now, each and every one of you will get sucked in but stay strong and focus on the mission. We realise the gravity of what we are asking and understand it will not be an easy mission but if anybody can do it, it's you fine ladies and gentlemen. I commend you.'

Garth tipped his satin top hat and blew kisses to all of them.

Danni felt a mixture of pride and dread. They had to succeed; the fate of the world depended on it.

Asterion tapped Garth gently on the back. 'Lovely sentiments indeed. We are so proud of you and have the utmost faith in your abilities. If I can give you any parting advice…bring it back to the heart. No matter how much they try to break, divide and push you, look inside yourselves and be strong. Your maturity and strength is light years beyond theirs just by standing as one at this very moment. Trust in yourselves and in each other. We will be here if you need guidance but predominantly this is something you must do as a team and as individuals. Good luck, Astro A Team. Your destiny is written in the stars…'

PART II

THE COUNTERPARTS

Chapter 4

Two against Two

'Dan, I love you but you look ridiculous!'

Danni threw her pillow at chuckling Drew before letting out an elongated, dramatic sigh. Her stomach was already queasy and a different kind of nausea arose from just looking at her bright yellow leggings and tank top in the mirror.

'This outfit says "bad '70s workout" not "save the world from complete destruction". How are the counterparts supposed to take me seriously looking like a spandex banana?'

Hannah appeared more sympathetic than her boyfriend who couldn't look at his best friend without doubling over in laughter.

'It doesn't look so bad, Danni. At least you and Charlotte can be a pair of bananas.'

She smiled wanly and pointed to Charlotte who was over at the breakfast buffet in a mustard playsuit and strappy heels for some silly reason.

'Gosh, she thinks everything is a fashion show,' Danni scoffed. 'I am definitely over Crawford but I have no idea what he sees in her.'

She couldn't understand how Charlotte could dress so uncomfortably and impractically for such an important mission. She also couldn't comprehend that Charlotte was eating breakfast. Last night after Garth and Asterion had left, the Astro A Team had moved their beds into a giant circle and stayed up well past midnight pigging out on the vast array of buffet food and drinks. They came up with many plans and strategies to tackle their mission and whilst it was confronting, Danni had enjoyed feeling so close to her team. She had tried to make eye contact with Reilly whenever either of them spoke but she noticed the Sagittarian was purposely avoiding her gaze. It was starting to become unbearable and Danni found herself constantly blinking back tears. It was hard to track time in the cave but it was about 2am when they finally fell asleep and none of them had stirred until the smells of cooked breakfast wafted under their noses. Danni had eaten enough the previous night to last her a lifetime.

The overall strategy concocted by the group was to send one person at a time into their Coloured Cavern rather than all at once so they could have a quick debrief before sending the next person through. It was almost like working in shifts and as Danni was the leader...three guesses who was going first. They had also decided to go in for one hour at a time. This was for two reasons. The first: everybody would have a chance to face their counterpart in one day with debriefs and meals in between. The second: they could get in, make their cases and have some discussion before leaving. They were aware the counterparts would try to manipulate them and lead them off course so an hour was enough time to stay on track and maintain their sanity. The group had also gone around in a circle and laid out exactly how they thought their counterpart would manipulate them. Danni and Charlotte agreed their less than fondness for one another would play a giant part. She knew it was important to bond with Charlotte but there was so much animosity between them and her "twin" wasn't exactly initiating peace either. When it came to Reilly's turn she mumbled, 'I know exactly what my counterpart is going to say and I'll handle it myself.'

Danni hung her head. She was praying the Sagittarian counterpart would somehow help Reilly soften towards her but she highly doubted it.

Ambrite briefly mentioned her negligent parents, leaving out her suicide attempt. Hunter relayed his story with an openness that Danni could tell the group appreciated. Graham said he was expecting to deal with a homophobic scorpion, which made the team laugh. Parry figured her beauty would be used against her and Hannah said she was terrified a giant crab would crush her with his pincers.

'Let's not forget Asterion said some of the counterparts were more placid,' Ronan appealed.

This set off further discussion about which of them would get lucky and which would be the worst to face-off against.

'So you're saying an angry sheep trumps a charging bull?' Ambrite had snorted at Hunter.

'Ram not sheep! And yes! The thing has horns!'

They had all agreed Brodie's would be the most intriguing. Of all the zodiac, her symbol was neither man nor beast.

'Am I seriously going to be chatting to a pair of scales?' the easy-going Libran had joked.

Crawford had barely uttered two words and Danni figured he was terrified about encountering a ferocious lion.

It didn't matter how much they plotted and theorised, they all knew they were in over their heads and would probably get sucked in as Garth had predicted before they could pull themselves together.

Now it was nearly time to begin the mission. Danni stood in front of the Cavern of the Yellow inspecting the luminous arch. She didn't hear Reilly approach from behind and jumped when she felt a light tap on her shoulder.

'Sorry,' Reilly muttered looking nervous. 'I just wanted to say good luck and I think you're brave volunteering to be first.'

Danni had to restrain herself from flinging her arms around her best friend. Instead, she smiled gratefully.

'Thank you. I'll be okay and as soon as I'm out I'll fill the group in with every detail.'

Reilly nodded and walked off. She may not have said much but it was a start and gave Danni the confidence she needed before entering.

The group including Charlotte began to walk over to Danni and one by one they all wished the pair good luck. Charlotte appeared bored by the whole ordeal. Danni turned to Drew and Hannah giving them both a hug and Ronan squeezed her shoulder. Charlotte chose to suck face with Crawford and once again Danni was thankful she had opted out of eating breakfast that morning.

She cleared her throat, impatiently waiting for Charlotte to join her. They stood side by side and Danni turned to address the group.

'Astro A Team...this is it. In exactly an hour, Charlotte and I will be back and we will go over everything we learnt so the next person is somewhat prepared. As we agreed last night, no one is permitted to enter their Cavern until we have returned. If for some reason we are not back after the hour is up, I would ask that you try to contact Garth or Asterion to check on us but don't come looking. Asterion mentioned that the mere sight of someone who is not the counterpart's astrological sign will set them off and we want to succeed. So relax, enjoy and we will see you very soon.'

The group broke into applause including Reilly. Danni and Charlotte turned to face their destiny. With a deep inhalation, they walked through the darkness…

*

The tunnel was pitch black and smelled musty. Every now and then, Danni could see the Gemini symbol ♊ etched on the wall and she mentally mapped those markers to guide the way. Charlotte kept letting out squeals as she slipped this way and that on the moist path. Danni was about to shush her when Charlotte screamed and fell onto Danni bringing them both hurtling to the ground. Danni banged her funny bone and let out a painful laugh. She immediately picked herself up and pulled Charlotte next to her.

'Why in the hell did you wear heels? Nobody cares what you look like here.'

'Save it, freak! You're the last person I would take fashion advice from. Plus Crawford cares and he is the love of my life so why don't you go back to tongue wrestling with that pretty blond boy of yours?'

Danni was about to trip Charlotte over again when she heard what sounded like the clashing of swords and loud grunts. Charlotte had heard it as well and without thinking, grabbed her hand and led them deeper into the tunnel. Her twin didn't let go; in fact she squeezed tightly and together they navigated through the darkness until a bright light flashed in the distance. The sound of metal meeting metal was becoming louder and Danni felt her heart begin to pump. She was about to meet her counterparts. As they drew closer, the light became blinding. The girls shielded their eyes, inching forward until they found themselves in a warm, yellow room double the size of their Mission Base. To say it was breathtaking was an understatement. Bookcases lined the entire right side of the room, filled with ancient tomes probably protecting archaic secrets. A bridge in the distance looked like it was made of solid gold and the river running under it sparkled and glinted. Danni wondered if the river was infused with starlight.

To the left, a giant wooden stand held various implements of torture. A colossal spiky mace lay wrapped in its chain at the bottom. Danni noticed throwing stars, daggers, a samurai sword boasting a hilt encrusted with garnets, pikes and dozens of other weapons hanging from the stand or leaning against the wall. Charlotte was already searching for the cavern exit. The girls had nowhere to run. A booming voice rang out from the centre of the room.

'You cannot leave! You are forever our prisoners!'

Sure enough, the exit was now blocked off and Danni began to sweat. They were only supposed to be in this room for an hour, not forever. She turned to Charlotte for support but the girl had lost all composure, staring at the two figures that had materialised in front of them.

Danni followed her gaze, her jaw dropping.

The twins were identical and appeared to be young adults. One had short, golden hair and green eyes whilst the other sported wavy black hair and piercing blue eyes. They were tall, sculpted and wearing open yellow shirts that revealed smooth tanned skin and a six pack that made body builders look puny. In short…they were so perfect it hurt.

Grinning, they looked at one another and took their shirts off. They were left standing in nothing but tailored skinny jeans. Charlotte whimpered and Danni fantasised for a micro second about the pros of being their prisoners. She was looking at Calvin Klein underwear models.

Why hadn't Garth warned them about how delicious their counterparts were?

She shook her head and tried to avoid looking directly at the brothers. This was all part of their manipulation to throw them off course and she was getting sucked in already. She turned to Charlotte and grabbed her hand again.

'Charlotte, stop looking at them. This is a trap to keep us here and forget about our mission. Let's try and speak to them diplomatically.'

Charlotte shook her hand off, mesmerised, and walked towards the twin with golden hair. Clearly she'd already chosen her favourite.

He stepped forward smiling and Danni watched Charlotte extend her hand and run it over his washboard abs. Danni felt jealous for a second before Charlotte let out a noise that sounded like air escaping from a balloon and fainted. She ran over, knelt down and began shaking her.

'Wake up, you lunatic! I can't do this without you!'

Charlotte lay flat and lifeless with no sign of regaining consciousness anytime soon. Danni stood, glaring at the twins who were still grinning.

'What have you done to her? Wake her up so we can talk to you both. We need to leave here in less than ten minutes. Wait — that can't be right!'

She couldn't believe how stupid they had all been. Time didn't work the same way on this planet. The one hour idea was absolutely pointless! She shook the watch she had borrowed from Graham off of her wrist and slipped it down her top.

The twins exchanged glances and turned back to Danni shaking their heads. The one with wavy black hair spoke, his eyes flashing like shiny sapphires.

'Like we said…you are forever our prisoners. Now feel free to make yourself at home. We were in the middle of a duel before you rudely interrupted our practice.'

With that, they ran up to the bridge, picked up their rapiers and began fencing. Danni stared at them in wonder, their bodies glistening as they jumped around weaving and dodging one another's cuts and thrusts.

Do they just swordfight all day looking hot? She took a deep breath and looked down at Charlotte. Danni was starting to panic. This had all started off so badly. They hadn't even been here ten minutes and already she was one man down. If they didn't leave soon, the group would worry and send for Asterion or Garth which would be super embarrassing after day one. Plus, she didn't want to face Garth's smugness regarding the time issue. She brushed a lock of hair from Charlotte's face and for the first time, wished she could talk to her. Straightening up, Danni raced towards the weapon stand. Settling on a rusty spear, she picked it up with one hand and felt the strain in her muscles from the weight. Gripping the base in her fist, she raised it over her head and ran to the bridge.

'Hey!' Danni stopped in front of the brothers who were now wrestling playfully.

They looked up, all sweaty and luscious from their activities. They stared at her for a second before snorting and grabbing each other in a headlock. Danni felt ridiculous. She must've looked like a gymnast in her exercise gear with a spear above her head.

'Wake her up and let us leave now before I turn you into a tasty kebab!'

She sounded braver than she felt. It wasn't in the mission to murder her counterparts who were clearly immortal anyway.

They broke apart, looking incredibly irritated. The dark-haired twin strode over to her, grabbed the spear and bent it as easily as a twig before throwing it over the bridge. He then performed an impressive backflip off the bridge into the sparkling stream below. His brother followed suit. Danni wished she could join in the fun and forget about the mission, her friendship with Reilly and her life back on Earth.

She walked down the bridge and sat on the edge of the riverbank. The twins ignored her and competed at who could handstand underwater the longest. She took her shoes off and gently placed a toe in the water. It was incredibly warm and soothing. With both feet submerged, she lay back, basking in the glow of the yellow cave. Her eyes became heavy and a deep sleep threatened to take over. The group would have called Garth or Asterion to check up on them by now wouldn't they? What if they were trapped here for eternity? There was no point trying to reason with the twins. They were too strong, too powerful and she was clearly outnumbered. Drowsy, she wandered over to the bookcases and pulled out a book with a golden spine. The title read *The Prowess of the Geminian Gods*.

Danni sniggered. Did they really believe they were gods? Sure, they looked the part but they were arrogant and cruel. They were giving Geminis a bad name. No wonder they were fighting with the rest of the counterparts; they clearly felt the most entitled to rule. Danni remembered one of the meetings where the Astro A Team had revealed the back stories behind the constellations. The Gemini Twins had names. Perhaps they would answer to them? They evidently revered knowledge judging by the number of books they owned. Danni put the book back in its place and ran to the river where the twins were splashing each other like children and laughing.

'I was just wondering which one is Castor and which is Pollux?'

The sounds of splashing ceased and both brothers turned to look at Danni with fury in their eyes.

Crap!

She took a few steps back as they rose out of the water and stormed over with menacing glares. The golden-haired twin grabbed Danni by her top and shook her until her teeth rattled.

'Don't you ever call us those names again, you ignorant Earth spawn! You stand here in yellow and claim to be a Gemini? You cannot even get along with your twin. You have been enemies since day one so forget everything that old man told you and keep out of our way!'

He threw her to the floor and lifted his foot, ready to crush her nose. Danni screamed.

'THAT IS ENOUGH!'

Danni craned her neck to see Asterion striding over to where she lay breathless and terrified.

The twins stepped away from Danni and picked up their rapiers, pointing them at the Keeper of the Stars.

'Stand back old man!' The dark-haired twin rotated the tip of his rapier and balanced on the balls of his feet.

Asterion sighed and waved his hand, snapping both rapiers in half. He held out his hand to Danni and pulled her up. She was still shaking as he strode over to Charlotte and revived her with a click of his fingers. She looked incredibly disoriented as he walked her over to Danni and positioned himself in front of them as a guard.

'Absolute power corrupts absolutely, Pollux,' Asterion warned the dark- haired twin.

'You have no right to call us by that name!' Pollux snarled.

'Actually I do, I named you, let's not forget.'

The golden-haired twin who was obviously Castor pulled on his shirt and handed the other to Pollux.

'Our mother was bewitched by you! You may have mated with her but that does not make you our father. Let it be known that Gemini will rule the Stars! Now take these pathetic children and leave us be.'

With that, the twins walked over the bridge and disappeared.

Danni stared in confusion. Asterion was Castor and Pollux's father? In Greek Mythology, Zeus had deceived the maiden Leda by transforming into a beautiful swan and mating with her. The Gemini twins were born as a result of their love affair.

'I know what you are thinking right now, Danni and I apologise for not telling you earlier about my connection to the twins. They have never viewed me as their real father but rather a man who took a fancy to their mother. I loved Leda but they don't seem to realise that. And to answer your question…I am not Zeus. That was just your planet's interpretation of events. I never turned into a swan either. I just loved her and she died giving birth to them. I honoured her by giving them such important roles to play but sadly they want nothing to do with me.'

Danni had so many more questions but she was still so shaken up from the attack, she hung her head. Charlotte looked green and ran to the river to be sick. Asterion patted her arm when she returned.

'Let me take you back to the base now. The group have been so worried and we need to have another big debrief before anybody enters those Coloured Caverns again.'

Chapter 5

The Archer

Reilly didn't want to admit she was worried. If she did, that meant she had forgiven Danni and she wasn't ready to let go of her anger yet. Still, her former best friend and Charlotte had been gone for a long time and the entire group were fearing the worst. They were only supposed to be gone an hour. What if something had happened and they had never made up? She shook her head…everything would be fine. Asterion had appeared after the group had started yelling for him and Garth to come to their aid and without saying anything, he had disappeared through the Cavern of Yellow. Now they were all sitting against the cave walls waiting for his return.

'I'm sure she's okay, Reilly,' her cousin reassured her.

Reilly smiled weakly at Hannah. 'I know…it's just scary. If their first attempt went badly, how are the rest of us going to go?'

Drew sidled over and draped his arm around her like they used to do in primary school. He signalled for Hannah to come closer and pulled her in on the other side.

'Ah, my two favourite ladies,' he crooned. Hannah giggled and Reilly rolled her eyes as she lay her head on his shoulder.

'We need to not get ahead of ourselves. Some of the counterparts are placid but Danni and Charlotte obviously drew the short straw. From what Asterion said, they sound like the most manipulative counterparts of them all. You might go in and have your hair braided by a centaur, you never know!'

Reilly snorted. 'I highly doubt it! He or she is going to torment me about being rejected by Slade and how my "best friend" betrayed me. I get to live all of those emotions over again...fun.'

Drew shifted nervously.

'What? Just say it.'

'It's just...she is so sorry, Reill! It was a stupid mistake and she knows it. I can't stand my two best friends not speaking to each other. Can't you just make up? How are you going to unite your team if you aren't united?

'Ugh, you sound like Garth now,' Reilly groaned.

Drew tipped an imaginary top hat which made her laugh.

'I hate this just as much as you, Drew but she betrayed me. She humiliated me in front of everybody when she should've just told me she had feelings for Slade. I would've backed down. I knew he liked her more and it really was just a silly crush. I want to forgive her but every time I think about it, it hurts so much. Best friends aren't supposed to do that to each other, period.'

Drew nodded and kissed the back of Hannah's hand. She loved watching her best friend treat her cousin like a princess. It was the little things he said or did that let Reilly know they would be together always.

'You take as long as you like and feel every feeling but please don't shut her out forever. She's just finding her way.'

Reilly wanted to protest, her pride forcing her to stay trapped in anger, but before she could open her mouth Asterion walked through the cave entrance. She stood up to see Danni straggling behind, her arm supporting Charlotte who looked deathly pale and miserable. Parry jumped up and nearly bowled everybody over, flinging her arms around Danni. Drew, Ronan and Hannah gave her gentler hugs which made Reilly spark with jealousy. That would've been her had the circumstances been different but she was glad to see Danni had some support. Ambrite and Hunter had been throwing her sympathetic glances since they'd arrived in

Bastion and she knew they weren't overly warm towards the Gemini just yet.

Asterion sat in his throne and once again beckoned to the Astro A Team to sit around him as they had done in the briefing. Reilly noticed Garth was absent from their meeting and was somewhat relieved. She knew Asterion would stick to the point, unlike his crazy Chief Advisor. Danni and Charlotte sat closest to him, unable to smile and looking traumatised. She wanted to hug and comfort Danni but that meant forgiving her. She knew Drew was right; she couldn't stay this way forever…

Asterion began to speak, breaking her train of thought.

'I have gathered you all to discuss exactly what happened when Danni and Charlotte entered the Cavern of Yellow and what measures the Astro A Team should take from now on to prevent something like this occurring again.'

He looked to Danni and Reilly watched her legs shake as she stood.

Danni faced the group and relayed exactly what had gone on in the Cavern of Yellow. When she reached the part about her attack, Reilly gasped. Their eyes met and Reilly saw how happy Danni looked upon hearing her concern. She quickly looked away as the cave exploded into a cacophony of yelling and questions.

'We have to abort this mission! It's too dangerous!' Slade shouted.

'Danni you are so brave! Thank you for trying,' Brodie added.

Reilly watched Ambrite and Hunter shuffle over and check to see if she was okay. Even they had forgiven her. Crawford was trying to subdue Charlotte who couldn't stop crying and blubbering.

'I love you, Craw, they meant nothing to me...it was a spell; their bodies were magical!'

Danni looked less miserable now; the colour returning to her cheeks.

'I told Asterion before we came back here that nothing and nobody in the world could stop me from going back in. We will succeed in this mission. We just need to be smarter about our approach.'

The cave erupted in protests once more. Reilly wasn't comfortable with Danni going back. It made her realise how much she cared and didn't want to lose her.

Asterion clapped his hands for order and silence.

'Danni is right. You will need to come up with a better plan otherwise you may not be as lucky as her. Your idea of going in for only an hour is silly. Time does not work the same way here, so Graham, your watch is useless.'

Danni pulled a Rolex out of her bra and tossed it at the Scorpio.

'The counterparts are unpredictable and don't care about your time sensitive mission. They may wish to keep you for longer and torment you or they may respond positively and if it's going well, you shouldn't leave after an hour anyway. Stay and make as much progress as you can. Also, if you all go in one at a time, you are taking a big risk. Try to enter the Coloured Caverns at the same time and return when it feels right.

'I will impose stricter security so none of you will be subjected to what Danni and Charlotte just went through. Garth has a dragon pendant he has been using to monitor you all since he found Danni. And before you begin protesting, he is not a stalker or using it in an unsavoury manner. It has been for your own safety and to keep you together. He will monitor all of you through the power of his dragon and if it appears any of you are in danger, we will appear and take you back. Do these sound like agreeable terms?'

Reilly's stomach rumbled in response. She was always so hungry, especially when nervous. She remembered gorging on food at the Astrological Dance after Slade had rejected her and cringed. Slade had barely spoken to her after that. She had to watch him lust after her best friend without any idea the feeling was mutual. Did Danni really like him that much? She didn't speak to him at all now and didn't seem that cut up about it. Maybe Slade had been a rebound after Crawford had rejected her.

And what was with Ronan fawning over her now? As long as Reilly could remember, Danni had never been interested in dating and now in the space of a year she had drawn the attention of three really good-looking boys. When was it her turn? Was she doomed to spend the rest of her life being the sidekick who liked to eat?

She was so lost in her own thoughts she didn't notice Asterion had vanished and the group were still crowded around Danni and Charlotte asking a million questions in hopes of preparing themselves for what lay ahead. She didn't want to prepare herself. She just wanted to walk in and experience it. She was actually looking forward to escaping the group for a while and having something to focus on.

Reilly heard Danni mention the names Castor, Pollux and something about Asterion being their father but that didn't sound right. Without alerting anybody, Reilly walked silently to the Cavern of Purple and stepped through…

*

I can't believe I just did that. What if I've worried them? What if they think I'm an attention seeker? Oh well. Too late to turn back now.

Reilly trudged through the dark tunnel following the lit up Sagittarian symbols ♐ and feeling progressively more nervous as she went along. After a couple more twists and turns she began to smell incense. It wafted through the passageway and burned her nostrils. Was it sandalwood? She was pretty sure it was sandalwood. Her mother loved that scent. Reilly missed her terribly. The aroma became stronger as she entered the most beautifully decorated purple room. It was as if she had stepped into a New Age store only this one came with a balcony that overlooked a lush green forest. Was the forest an illusion? How could it fit into the cave? Reilly wandered over and let her fingers brush the chimes hanging from the ceiling. They tinkled playfully. This was the most calming, beautiful place she had ever seen. She spotted the incense burning on the hand of a large, stone centaur. In the centre of the room, lay a velvet rug with dozens of soft pillows in all different colours. She lay amongst them and stretched out her legs. *My counterpart has amazing taste…*

Reilly turned her head this way and that marvelling at the spiritual accents that covered every surface of the cave. A rumbling noise made her clutch her stomach but it wasn't hunger. The sound belonged to hooves thundering somewhere between the trees. Reilly stood and walked to the balcony, noticing the hidden wooden walkway that spiralled down into the forest. The clip clop of the hooves increased. Out of the thicket, a gorgeous centaur appeared. Reilly stared in awe as he trotted up the walkway with a quiver full of arrows strapped to his back and a bow in his left hand. *What could he possibly be hunting out there?*

She remembered how Danni was attacked and took a few steps backward but stopped when their eyes met. His face was rugged and unshaven, with amethyst eyes and coffee-coloured hair. His torso was perfectly sculpted with just the right amount of chest hair and his lower body was…well, a horse. She felt it wrong to find him so attractive but he *was* half a man and in her view that was a glass half full!

He smiled warmly and lay his bow down on the bench. Unstrapping his quiver, he let it slide to the floor, allowing arrows to spill out in every direction. She looked away shyly despite the fact he was already naked. He was pure perfection and once again someone she couldn't be with…

'Hello, Reilly Julia Chase,' he said. 'Welcome to the Cavern of Purple. Please, I've been expecting you.'

Her face turned bright red. Only her mother addressed her in this way and it was always used in a negative context. He made it sound so…sexy.

'Ummm…thank you. What can I call you?'

'You may call me Chiron but please do not confuse me with the Greek Mythology your planet invented. I did not teach Hercules nor partake in epic battles. I am simply a centaur that rules Sagittarius and hopefully soon Bastion.'

Reilly drew in a breath. This was her moment.

'Why do you believe you should rule over the other counterparts?'

Chiron cocked his head to the side. 'Because I am an ancient creature that is infinitely wise and philosophical. Who could run Bastion better than I? The goat believes himself to be the most logical but his weakness lies in his negativity. If you're going to rule you must be optimistic and enjoy the responsibility.'

Reilly made a mental note to tell Ronan about his depressing goat when she returned. Chiron spoke so well and convincingly she nearly agreed with his argument before stopping herself.

'Well, yes but isn't it much wiser and more spiritual to share the power with your fellow counterparts rather than keep it for yourself?'

'You speak like a true Sagittarian,' he grinned. 'I quite like your robe.'

She looked down at her purple tie-dye dress. It was her favourite piece in the wardrobe and hugged her curvy figure nicely.

Is he flirting with me?

'How does a true Sagittarian speak?' asked Reilly.

'Diplomatically, honestly and with much virtue. Don't you see this is why our star should rule? Have you met the other counterparts? No, of course you haven't. Well they are fools, the lot of them. The crab is terrified of her own shadow and the maiden cares only for her image.'

Reilly couldn't believe how much she was already getting out of their conversation. She wanted to take notes. This was the complete opposite of how Danni's encounter had gone. Finally, something was going her way for once…

'I agree you are well-spoken and would make a great ruler but you have to consider the company you keep. Each counterpart balances the other out with their strengths and weaknesses. I'm sure you have a weakness. Mine is emotional eating.'

In an instant, Chiron's smile faded as he regarded her with disgust.

'Is that why Slade chose Danni over you? You eat too much, who would desire that?'

Reilly was completely taken aback. Her face turned red and she felt incredibly self-conscious. She was no longer calm in a peaceful place. Even though she had been expecting something to this effect it still drove a knife right through her. How could someone so charming become so cold in an instant? At least the Gemini twins were "douchey" from the beginning.

'I don't see what that has to do with anything!'

Chiron laughed and clomped his hooves on the wooden floors.

'It is extremely relevant. You are a representative from Earth, are you not? You are an immature child that is not desired by anybody. If Danni was a Sagittarius, she would have made a much better representative than you. At least she has been lusted after.'

'No! Stop it!'

'You are not worthy of any man. A man cannot love one that does not love herself.'

Reilly blocked her ears and kept repeating, 'I don't care, I don't care.' But she did and when the tears finally came, they did not stop. She crumbled and buried her face in the soft cushions, sobbing. She couldn't take it anymore. Everything she had been feeling since the night they left Earth poured out of her. Danni's betrayal, her rejection, her insecurities and the humiliation. She cried until her throat was raw and she was physically exhausted. Looking up through blurred eyes, she realised the room was empty. Chiron had left her completely alone. In the distance, she could hear hooves cantering through the forest becoming fainter and fainter. Sitting up, she deliberately blew her nose on his rug and rubbed her eyes on the cushions, leaving splotches of black makeup.

'Are you okay, sweetheart?'

She whirled around to see Garth looking concerned.

Of course, he would've seen the whole thing through the power of his dragon necklace.

Reilly honestly thought she couldn't cry any more tears but seeing his empathetic expression set her off again. Garth knelt down and cradled her in his arms. She was so grateful for the affection, she clung to him and wept.

'Shhhh,' he soothed. 'Reilly, you are such a beautiful girl and person, don't even think on it for a second. Chiron was purposely trying to hurt you and it worked.'

'I know,' she gulped. 'It was building up and he knew just what to say to make me crumble.'

'You need to make up with Danni, my love, it's killing you. You won't succeed if you don't have the support from your best friend.'

Reilly pulled back and looked into his warm, chocolate eyes. He smiled and used a thumb to wipe some of her smudged mascara.

'I want to but I still can't get over how easy it was for her to kiss Slade. Does fifteen years of friendship really mean nothing to her?'

Garth released her and crossed his legs on the rug. Reaching into his white shirt, he pulled out the chain with the silver dragon hanging from it. Holding the chain between his forefinger and thumb he let the dragon swing back and forth. Reilly stared in fascination as its eyes began to glow and the room started to hum. Garth had his eyes closed and was muttering something under his breath. The glow grew into a blinding flash resulting in a clear image projecting itself on the wall. He opened his eyes and turned to Reilly.

'I have never shown anybody besides Asterion the power of my necklace but I'm going to show you exactly what happened the day Danni and Slade kissed.'

Reilly took a deep breath and focused on the screen. She saw Danni looking disgruntled in her living room. She watched Danni answer the doorbell, trying to brush Slade off until he insisted they talk. She watched them sitting closely on the couch holding hands and heard Danni protest that she was Reilly's best friend and it would be wrong to take things further. Her heart sank as she watched Slade throw himself at Danni and awkwardly watched them kiss for a while. The image suddenly shifted and Reilly saw Charlotte smirking and filming them through the window on her phone before running off. Garth shook his head, clucking his tongue. Slade was now spooning Danni and her former best friend looked horrified. Reilly witnessed the moment Danni realised what she had done. She watched intently as Danni told Slade she was a horrible person and they could never be more than friends. He told her he was disappointed but admired her loyalty. Slade got up and exited the house. Reilly watched Danni slump onto the couch with her head in her hands. The dragon let out a roar and the image vanished, its eyes no longer glowing.

Garth cleared his throat.

'I wanted you to see this because yes, they did kiss, there is no denying it but Danni did not enjoy herself and it wasn't as easy as you thought. She is still punishing herself for what she did and always will. You have to remember Danni was deeply hurt by her own betrayal from Crawford. She felt vulnerable and as you can see, Slade was incredibly persistent. It was an honest mistake and one I know she will never repeat.'

Reilly leaned in and kissed Garth on the cheek. He blushed and tipped his hat.

'Thank you for showing me this. I feel so much better now. But what do I do about Chiron?'

He rose to his feet, pulling her up alongside him.

'That is something you'll have to figure out. There is no set rule for each of the counterparts. They all respond positively and negatively to different things just as all of you in the Astro A Team do. Return to the heart and make all your decisions from there. Leave logic out of this one is all I can say.'

Reilly nodded. Next time she would be more prepared.

Chapter 6

The Castle in the Sea

She was beautiful and vibrant. His damsel in distress. A maiden fair with long red hair. Nothing and nobody would ever come between them.

Drew strummed an imaginary guitar with the pick he kept on a string around his neck.

'My lovely muse has inspired me to sing about her white cape.'

Hannah giggled. 'It's a kimono, baby. It's in right now.'

'Kimono? Isn't that what geishas wear? Well, I admire a girl who keeps up with the latest fashions even on another planet.'

He poked her in the ribs and smiled as she giggled.

'You're an adorable Poppin Fresh. I'm going to call you that from now on!'

Danni groaned and Drew chuckled.

'I forgot you were there, Dan, sorry!'

'How can you guys be so mushy when your best friend entered her Coloured Cavern without even saying anything?'

Drew scratched his head.

'You know, I've been mediating between the both of you all day. I reassured her you would be fine and now I'm reassuring you that *she* will be fine.'

'Was she worried about me?' Danni squeaked, her pitch high and hopeful.

'She was indeed and I know she wants to be friends again. She's just torn but the girl is cracking and I'll break her yet.'

'Thanks, Drew. Did you know she wished me good luck before I entered my Coloured Cavern?'

Drew whistled. Having two female best friends could be intense but he wouldn't have it any other way. It had taught him to be sensitive and hopefully a good boyfriend to Hannah.

'I did not but that is an excellent sign. I'm going to leave as soon as Reilly gets back.'

As if he'd conjured her, Reilly stepped through her Coloured Cavern and walked over to them. He noticed she had been crying and stood up with arms outstretched. She fell into them and he squeezed her tightly. Danni and Reilly used to jokingly compete for who was Drew's favourite and in all honesty he couldn't choose. They were both wonderful and special to him in their own way. In fifteen years he had never wanted anything more from them; they were his girls but never his girlfriends.

Hannah rubbed Reilly's shoulder and Drew noticed Danni standing at a distance unsure of how to act.

Reilly released him and turned to all of them.

'I'll tell you guys everything that happened but right now I need to talk to Hannah about her counterpart and Ronan and Parry if they are around?'

'Parry's gone in but Ronan is here somewhere,' said Hannah. 'Let's go chat on my bed.'

Drew grabbed her hand as she got up to leave with Reilly.

'My white dove, I am going in now too. Don't leave without saying goodbye.'

His girlfriend turned and threw her arms around his neck. She pressed her soft lips against his. He melted. *How does she do it?*

'Stay safe, snuggly bear!'

Hannah kissed him once more and walked off with Reilly.

Drew stared after her with his mouth open. She could have had a beard down to her toes and he would still be in awe of her. Danni waved a hand in front of his face, snapping him out of it.

'Snuggly bear, I'm off to have a chat with Charlotte. Hopefully after our horrific experience we can bond a little more. Good luck and don't offend the fishes!'

She gave him a quick hug and walked off.

Drew felt a lump in his throat. *Mr Puffer Snuggles…I hope someone is looking after him…*

He turned to gaze at the enormous aquarium next to the Cavern of Sea Foam. It was the most beautiful and mesmerising thing he had ever seen…apart from Hannah. Fish of all colours and sizes darted this way and that. Drew had spent a lot of his life reading up on marine life and these fish were unlike any species he had ever researched. The gigantic stone castle in the middle was planted firmly in the sand. It had an air of majesty to it. Drew began initiating staring competitions with all the fish that swam past in case they were his counterparts. After a while his head began to throb from staring through a pane at glassy fish eyes and figured they would be waiting inside the castle. He stepped through the Cavern of Sea Foam, passing the symbols of Pisces ♓ until he came to a stop in front of a wooden drawbridge.

He could smell the seawater and wondered whether he should've changed into sea foam board-shorts. Instead, he had opted for skinny jeans in the same colour and a plain V-neck t-shirt. He looked like *Gumby.* Drew passed through the drawbridge into the stone castle and gasped. It looked like something out of a video game he liked to play. The stone walls were decorated with the same brightly coloured seaweed in the aquarium. Conch shells lined all the closed doors around the centre of the main room. Drew craned his neck and noticed spiral staircases winding all the way to the ceiling with doorways hidden in every mossy niche. At the centre of the roof hung a crystal chandelier that resembled a jellyfish, its tentacles glittering and reflecting light. In front of him was a deep spherical pool that led out into the aquarium. The water looked so inviting he wanted to take a swim. He took a couple of steps and peered over the edge. A bright orange, eel -like creature swam past crackling with electricity. He jumped back and ran halfway up the stairs to one of the wooden doors and tried to open it but it wouldn't budge. *How do fish walk up the stairs and open doors anyway?*

He was about to give up when he heard giggles coming from the pool. As he peered down, two stunning mermaids emerged from the water and sat on the edge of the pool. One was Asian looking with long black hair and obsidian eyes. Her clam shell bra was bright red which matched her ruby lips and the tropical flower in her hair. The other had luminous golden hair that cascaded down to her navel. She had a blue clam shell bra, aqua lips and matching flower. Their bellies were flat and their tails shimmered and shone with gleaming green scales. There was no doubt Hannah was the love of Drew's life but the perky mermaids had certainly caught his attention. He steadied himself against the door and let out a long exhalation. Why couldn't they have been mermen or actual fish? Girls had always been his weakness and what man hadn't fantasised about a busty mermaid or two in his lifetime? They giggled once more and he looked down to see them smiling right at him. Without saying anything, they curled their fingers and gestured for him to come closer.

Oh Lordy, this is going to be a challenge!

Drew did his best not to fall down the steps, taking them one at a time with his hand against the stone wall to steady him. He must've looked like a massive loser. They were even more beautiful up close. He couldn't say which was more attractive; they were every man's dream. They gestured for him to sit on the edge and he did so, taking his socks and runners off. The pool was warm and soothing. He grinned as they clapped their hands in glee. The Asian mermaid looked him up and down with hungry eyes. He felt his face burn and let his ankles sink in deeper. The blonde mermaid gave what sounded like a purr as she trailed her fingers in the water.

'You are very pleasing to our eyes,' said the Asian mermaid. She wriggled closer. Drew shifted slightly back.

'Mmmm,' agreed the blonde. 'When we heard a boy from Earth was coming to speak with us, we begged Garth to bring us somebody handsome and he delivered.'

Drew choked on his own saliva. They weren't making things easy for him.

'Ahhh well, thank you for having me in your stony fortress of sexitude...I mean solitude! My name is Drew and you are?'

'My name is Calypsee and my sister is Sirena,' the Asian mermaid said. 'Have you brought gifts for us?'

They both stretched out their hands and batted their eyelashes.

Drew shoved his hands in his pockets hoping there was something he could give them. He figured if he gave them something they would be obliged to help him out. His skinny jeans were so tight he could barely fit a toothpick in there so he took the guitar pick that hung around his neck and offered it with reluctance.

The mermaids *oohed* and *aahed*, grabbing the tiny pick and sniffing it. They didn't seem too happy that there was only one gift between the two of them but they took it in turns to hold it and marvel. Drew stared at them in amusement. He had so many back home that snapped so easily they were hardly an item of value but they didn't know that. Sirena placed the pick down her cleavage for safe-keeping. Drew did his best not to stare.

'We are most pleased with your token from Earth. Will you take a swim with us?'

Calypsee reached over and tugged on his skinny jeans, meaning to take them off.

Drew jumped up, his face burning. 'Ahhh well, as a mortal human I cannot breathe underwater like you can. I'll drown!'

Sirena tilted her head in confusion. 'But you are the Pisces representative from Earth, are you not? Surely you have gills or sea-legs?'

'Oh I am indeed the Pisces representative. I have my own fish named Mr Puffer Snuggles and you should see me swim laps at Juggler's Corner Aquatic Centre but I have no gills or sea-legs. If I stay underwater for more than a minute, I'll begin to drown.'

Calypsee pouted. 'We knew you weren't a merman but we thought you would at least have gills. Never mind, we will stay and play with you here.'

Before Drew could protest, both mermaids advanced. Calypsee shuffled onto his lap, her bottom half quite heavy. She stroked his chest while Sirena sat behind him and massaged his shoulders. His eyes rolled back as he surrendered to their pampering.

What was I supposed to be doing again?

They kept giggling and whispering nonsensical things in his ear. It sounded like deep secrets of the ocean. Hands were pawing at him, lips were nicking the bare parts of his skin and hair was constantly being flicked into his eyes. The pleasure was overwhelming but it felt incredibly wrong. Drew closed his eyes and pictured Hannah kissing him, touching him the way she did. He felt a love so strong it forced him to push them off and jump to his feet. The mermaids blinked in surprise, their lipsticks smeared.

'Listen here, you sultry fishwives!' Drew shouted. 'I love my girlfriend Hannah! I love her so much I'm going to marry her and we are going to have lots of fishes...I mean babies! How dare you touch what isn't yours! You want some of this? Well you can't have it!'

He expected the mermaids to drown him in the pool but instead they erupted into sobs and wails. Clutching one another, Calypsee and Sirena howled and howled, shaking the castle walls. Their cries were so powerful Drew had to block his ears. The pool in the centre started to whirl rapidly in a clockwise direction. Drew edged backwards, ready to run through the drawbridge. The mermaids stopped crying and flashed him an evil glare. With a flick of their fins, they jumped into the whirlpool and caused a giant wave to emerge and crash over him. Drew braced himself but it didn't prevent him from getting absolutely saturated. He opened his eyes, his arms still shielding his body and noticed the mermaids had disappeared back into the aquarium. Peering over the edge, the same orange eel swam past and Drew shook his fist at it for no good reason.

Danni may have been attacked and Reilly may have cried but he hadn't even had a chance to discuss the mission. He was about to leave when he noticed the guitar pick lying at his feet. It must've fallen out of Sirena's bra when she was violating him. He picked it up and threaded it through the string around his neck. There wasn't much more he could do. He was completely drenched from head to foot. His skinny jeans were now wearing *him!* Drew turned to leave through the drawbridge and saw Garth sitting on the steps grinning at him.

'Yeah, laugh it up, dragon boy,' Drew snarled.

Garth put his hands up in a gesture of surrender.

'Hey, I'm not judging. We both have dark skin and the merbabes love a bit of brown sugar!'

'Yeah, well I feel horrible now. I know technically I didn't cheat but the fact I allowed them to manhandle me for even a second makes me feel unfaithful to Hannah.'

Garth clicked his fingers. Drew's entire body was instantly dry and warm. He bowed in gratitude.

'You did nothing wrong. They manipulated you just as I said they would. Do you think Sirena and Calypsee would've done that to anyone who walked through their castle? They know you've always had a weakness for the ladies and they preyed on that.'

'So...they didn't find me handsome?' Drew frowned.

'I'm sure they did but the counterparts look deep into your soul and play through your insecurities, weaknesses and shortcomings. If Graham had been a

Pisces, they would've told him chinos make his butt look big.'

Drew shook his head. 'That's pure evil.'

Garth chuckled. 'I've seen you with Hannah and nobody is more devoted to his girlfriend than you are. I don't think you should hide what happened. Tell her the truth. I was watching the entire time, I can vouch for you.'

Drew pursed his lips. 'I don't know why you're being so nice to me. I clearly failed my mission. As if they are going to have a logical discussion with me after I called them sultry fishwives. Danni told me not to offend the fishes and I did.'

Garth walked through the drawbridge and gestured for Drew to follow. Drew took one last look behind him at the pool and noticed Calypsee and Sirena propped up against the edge. Their hands were cupping their faces and they were pouting. He gave a small wave which caused them to swoon before diving back into the pool. Drew threw his hands up in confusion and ran after Garth.

'As you can see, you haven't failed,' said Garth. 'The mermaids don't have normal human emotions. They range from deliriously happy to extremely sad to murderous and back to happy again.'

'So basically like all women then?' Drew joked.

'They're actually quite harmless and just want to play,' Garth continued. 'You made them unhappy when you rejected them but they'll forgive and adore you again in an instant.'

'Women,' muttered Drew. 'Well, how am I supposed to succeed next time if they keep trying to undress me?'

Garth stopped just before the cave entrance. He put both hands on Drew's shoulders.

'I'll give you one piece of advice…ride the waves.'

Drew nodded although he had no idea what that meant. Garth tipped his hat and vanished. Drew stepped through the cave and saw Reilly and Hannah sitting on his bed talking. Danni and Charlotte were near the buffet munching on something and having what looked to be an intense conversation. He strode over to his bed and lovingly wrapped his arms behind Hannah.

She jumped and turned around. Flinging her arms around his neck, she squeezed him tightly.

'Tell me everything!'

Drew sucked in a deep breath.

'Reilly, do you mind if I talk to Hannah alone for a second?'

Reilly smiled and hugged her cousin before heading to the showers.

They sat cross-legged on his bed, facing one another. Holding both of her dainty hands, he spilled out the entire story. How the mermaids had thrown themselves at him. How he had fallen under their spell for a second before pushing them away and what Garth had told him afterwards. She remained calm the entire time he spoke and kissed him once he had finished. He felt relieved. He had been so terrified she would leave him.

'Baby, I know you love me and would never hurt me,' said Hannah. 'Asterion warned us we would be manipulated so I'm not mad at all. I hate their guts but you've done nothing wrong.'

Drew exhaled. She had taken it so well and a little jealousy was healthy; it meant she cared.

'I'm so glad because I feel terrible! They were all over me and used their feminine wiles to distract me but the second I closed my eyes and thought of you, I had the strength to push them away.'

Hannah stroked his cheek. 'I will murder them for that but for now I suggest you ride the wave like Garth suggested. If you're calm, they will be calm. If they cry then you cry too. Be the merman within.'

'I still have no idea what that means but I love you. Speaking of calm, I can't believe how well you've taken everything. You don't seem to be freaking out about facing your counterpart.'

Hannah was so excited she bounced up and down on the bed.

'Reilly told me everything that happened when she faced her counterpart. He sounds like a right ass but that's not the point. He let slip a few things about the other counterparts. He told her that the Virgo is obsessed with her own image which doesn't surprise me but unfortunately Parry had already left before Reilly could tell her. He told her the Capricorn goat is quite negative so she's going to fill Ronan in before he leaves and he told her that the Cancerian Crab is scared of her own shadow.'

Drew raised his eyebrows. 'Is that supposed to be a good thing?'

'Yes! It means that I get to be the brave one!' Hannah squealed. 'I was so scared I would be facing off against a gigantic killer crab and to know before I go in that she is a big scaredy crustacean is a huge advantage.'

Drew had always liked feeling the hero around Hannah. He was so used to her anxiety but seeing this newfound courage made him love her all the more.

'My dove, this is a chance for you to grow some confidence. You're right, this is a massive advantage. By coming out of your shell, you can help it come out too. Sorry…I couldn't help myself.'

'I know. I think I might be the first one to succeed but I won't get ahead of myself just yet. Will you walk me to the Cavern of White? I've been talking a lot with Reilly and I feel ready.'

'Of course.' Drew stood up and extended his hand. She clasped it and they walked to the Cavern of White. He turned and pulled her into his arms.

'I'm so proud of you, Hanny,' he whispered. 'People just see you as the scared girl with no backbone but you've got so much potential. Go show them what you're made of!'

'People think I have no backbone?'

'Thatta girl! Off you go!' Drew pushed Hannah into the Cavern of White. She shrieked as she crashed into the side wall.

'Ahhh who needs merbabes when you've got a classy gal like that?' Drew shook his head smiling.

Chapter 7

Returning to the Heart

Hannah rubbed her arm and glared at the back of her boyfriend who was now walking towards the buffet with his arms outstretched. A fiery resolve had awakened inside her.

I'll show them who has no backbone…

She put both hands on her slim waist and marched through the Cavern of White with determination. She was so grateful for the insight provided by her cousin. It gave her the courage she needed to brave the dark, musty cave with the Cancerian symbol ♋ lighting her way. The walls smelled like mildew and seaweed. It turned her stomach but she traipsed forward, hoping the crab wouldn't sneak up behind her. Hannah knew deep down that the Astro A Team probably saw her as pathetic and weak but there was a good reason why she was incredibly sensitive. She had been diagnosed with Generalized Anxiety Disorder when she was fifteen after her father was kicked out of the house for cheating on her mother. Since his departure, she had experienced strong and frequent bouts of panic, gasping for breath and rocking in the dark from nightmares she couldn't shake. It had been a lot better since she joined the Astro A Team and met Drew but it still lived deep within her nerves and sprang forth at the slightest threat.

She had only confided her deep dark secret to Reilly and Drew and hoped with all her heart that the counterpart wouldn't use it against her.

The fishy smell was becoming more and more pungent so Hannah blocked both sides of her nostrils with her index finger and thumb. A cold wind kissed her face as she entered a big blue cavern that opened up into a vast ocean. The calm dark water stretched for miles with no end in sight. It was hard to believe she was even in a cave anymore. The edge of the ocean was paved with soft sand and littered with brightly coloured seashells. Hanna kicked off her white flats and pressed her feet into the surprisingly warm sand. An icy wind kept billowing around and nipping at her bare skin. She pulled the sides of her kimono tightly around her and sat on the sand.

The brightly coloured shells were varied in shape and size. She picked up a glittering gold conch shell. There was something very familiar about them. It took a moment for her to realise they were all the colours of the zodiac. Hannah badly wanted to pocket the shell and take it home. This place was so surreal she needed the memento to remind her this had actually happened when they finally returned home. Taking a quick look around, she slipped the shell swiftly into her pocket. What was one shell? There were hundreds on the sand.

Suddenly she felt a tiny pinch on her foot. Hannah peered down and saw the cutest little white crab nipping at her with miniature pincers. It was so cute Drew would've picked it up and cuddled it like a baby. Hannah wasn't afraid of the small crustacean before her. She reached out and ran a finger over its hard outer shell. It appeared to shiver before disappearing back into its husk.

'Oh I'm sorry, little crab,' Hannah squeaked. 'I didn't mean to scare you. Please come back out...I'm Hannah, the Cancerian representative from planet Earth.'

The crab poked its head out and with astonishing speed scuttled sideways into the ocean. She stood and was about to run after it when the ocean began to rumble. The sand beneath her feet trembled. The shells jumped and danced in the air from the chaos in the sea. Hannah felt her mouth become dry. The thick black waves rose up and splashed down with brute force. The wind whipped around her, turning her fingernails blue and causing her teeth to chatter. Hannah slipped her feet back into her flats and ran back to the now closed cave entrance.

Backing herself up against the wall, she screamed as the waves began to crash onto the shore, sprinting up to kiss her toes. She pulled her white leggings up and waded to a corner that hadn't been hit yet. The waves were attacking the sand harder and faster now. Hannah was close to fainting from panic but she pushed herself to remain conscious on the basis that this was a matter of life and death. In a couple of minutes, the waves would reach her and she would drown. Where were Garth and Asterion? Weren't they going to save her? She felt something poke her sides and remembered the conch shell she had pocketed. With her last ounce of courage, she pulled the shell out.

'STOP,' she screamed, before throwing it as hard as she could back into the ocean. The shell buried itself deep beneath the blue. Hannah scrunched up her face as a giant wave came hurtling towards her.

This is it…Drew…it can't end like this…

Suddenly, the entire room became silent. Her body remained dry. Hannah opened her eyes and saw the ocean calm once more. The shells continued to glitter along the shore. It was as if nothing had ever happened. A burst of adrenaline ran through system. She leapt onto the sand in relief, happy to be alive. Shuffling her feet into the warm granules again, Hannah buried her face in her hands. That was the single most terrifying experience she had ever faced and yet it had helped her overcome extreme fear. She laughed hysterically.

If only the others could see I have backbone out the yin yang now!

Ready to leave, Hannah turned towards the cave entrance. The path was still closed in stone however a gigantic white crab now covered the entire length of the wall. Its body was predominantly snow white and it sported a smooth, ivory belly. Its pincers were coal black, shiny and menacing, resembling enormous tusks. Its bright red eyes were set far apart and evidently the smallest part of the phenomenal crustacean that was on display before her. Four solid legs were visible on either side of its body. Hannah watched in terror as they moved together slowly down the wall. It stared back with beady eyes. Her feet felt rooted in the sand. Her counterpart clicked its pincers loudly and Hannah fell backwards, the sand breaking her fall. She could swear it sniggered and nearly cried in frustration before remembering her conversation with Reilly.

Frowning, she rose to her feet and stared at the amused crustacean before jumping towards it with both arms outstretched like a zombie lusting for brains. The crab gave a high-pitched squeak and scuttled back onto the cave wall which sounded like a hundred typewriters being used at once. The click clack of its claws and legs hitting the stone was nearly deafening. This time, Hannah gave an exaggerated snigger and immediately felt bad as it continued to squeak in fright. She softened and gestured with her hand for it to come down.

'Please…I'm sorry. There is nothing to be frightened of. I'm a harmless girl who loves animals. I would never ever hurt you…not like you tried to hurt me before with the waves.'

The crab cautiously click clacked its way back to the sand. Hannah inched forward, bravely reaching out to stroke the shell. The crab froze but fortunately didn't dismember her hand. Surprisingly, it allowed to her to lovingly run her fingers along its rocky, white husk. She smiled as its beady eyes closed. Hannah began to croon a lullaby her mother would sing when she was having severe panic attacks.

'Don't be scared, it's okay, you're just having a bad day. Hold me tight, I'm right here and I will take away your fear. When the storm begins to pass, you will be home at last. So please don't frown and please don't cry. You precious darling child of mine.'

The crab opened its red eyes and without fear, spoke with the familiar voice of a gentle female. Her words sounded across the ocean and echoed in Hannah's ears.

'I love you…'

Hannah started in shock as tears came into her eyes. The crab sounded just like her mother and it had uttered those three words with such affection. Was it playing tricks on her?

'Mum…?'

'No…but I figured her voice would be the most comforting.'

Hannah was so touched she felt a lump lodge in her throat.

'Do you really love me?'

It nodded and nudged her gently. She giggled and stroked its shell again. It shivered in pleasure.

'You aren't like anybody I've ever met before. Are all people from Earth as kind as you?'

'Well, most people are and the others…I'm sure they want to be, they just don't know how.'

The crab gave a grunt that puffed sand into Hannah's face. She coughed and wiped her eyes.

'Sorry, Hannah, it's just the counterparts here are awful to me. They have absolutely no sensitivity. They find me weak and don't respect me. I may not be strong like the lion or skilled in combat like the twins but my love is as deep as an endless ocean and to me that is the most powerful weapon. Don't you agree?'

Hannah nodded.

'I understand and agree wholeheartedly. My group have never said it to my face but I know they think I have no backbone. So what if I'm anxious? I am kind and isn't that the most important quality in a person?'

The crab clicked its pincers with excitement. It was still very unnerving for Hannah who took a step back.

'Cancerians are the most loving and committed sign they say. Did you know why the Moon is our planet? Because we light the night with white. That is our shade as you know and wear so beautifully. We are pure, unselfish and kind. Why shouldn't we rule? Every decision we make would be the most sincere.'

Hannah sat back down and nestled her head against the crab's concrete leg.

'That is beautiful and yes I knew that about Cancerians but my boyfriend is a Pisces and he is one hundred per cent devoted to me. He is also very committed. I think that says more about his heart than his sign.'

The crab let out another squeak.

'I suppose you are right, Hannah. It's like you said, other people want to be kind but don't know how. Your boyfriend knows how and you certainly do but the counterparts do not. How do I make them love as we do?'

Hannah picked up one of the shells absent-mindedly and noticed the crab eyeing her. She quickly put it down and hid her blushing cheeks.

'I was never going to kill you, Hannah,' the crab explained. 'I was just scared when I saw you take my shell. It made me angry. I wanted to protect my home but it was wrong to frighten you as I did.'

Hannah looked up to see the crab was sincere.

'It's okay. I shouldn't have taken what wasn't mine. I'm sorry for scaring you. We are just a bunch of scaredy-cats.'

'Or crabs.' The crustacean swayed, mimicking laughter.

Hannah giggled. She drew a heart in the sand and pointed to it.

'The way to make the counterparts love as we do is to lead by example. No more trying to be right or the ruler. No more trying to compete. We just share our love and hope that they will love us and each other in return.'

'Is it really so simple?'

'Yes! Don't you see? Where there is war, there is no peace and love. If everybody believes they are right then nobody is right. Just like religion…'

The crab raised a pincer. 'Religion?'

'Never mind…the point is, nothing but devastation will hit Bastion if the counterparts keep fighting to rule. They, including you, need to learn to love and rule together as one.'

Hannah shook from the cold and exhaustion. She had endured so many extreme emotions in just an hour and it was starting to have an impact.

'You are cold. You should go and let me think on what you've said because I do love it and I do love you very much.'

Hannah smiled a watery smile.

'I love you too…ummm, what do I call you?'

'Karkinos or Karki if you like. Could you bring your boyfriend on your next visit? I would like to see human love.'

'Is he allowed to enter the Cavern of White when he's a Pisces?'

'Oh yes, I allow it. I'm not sure if he has met Sirena and Calypsee yet but the mermaids visit my ocean from time to time and dote on me. They are the only other counterparts I feel comfortable with.'

Hannah frowned. She was still trying to ignore the mental images of the lusty fishwives pawing at her man.

'They sound like real gems of the sea…'

'Indeed they are. Now return to the warmth, dear Hannah. We will work on this plan together in due time. It makes sense to me now…spread love not war.'

Hannah nodded. 'Yes, something like that.'

She made her way towards the exit but before stepping through, Hannah turned back to see Karki happily swaying back and forth.

'Do you know? About my life?'

'I do and I understand fear more than anybody,' said Karki.

'Fear is not weakness, Hannah, it is strength. You feel fear because you are so aware of the world around you and that is intelligence. Just try not to let it rule you or stop you from living a life full of adventure.'

Hannah bit her lip. 'I won't if you won't. Let's help each other, Karki.'

'Gladly. Maybe if we share love, we won't need to be afraid anymore.'

'I hope so.'

'Hannah?'

Karki raised its heavy pincer and she saw the golden conch shell resting on it.

Hannah skipped back down to the sand, picked up the shell and kissed Karki on its husk. The crab quivered in delight and shrunk to its miniature form again.

Hannah missed Karki the second she stepped through the exit. It had been like having her mother with her. She felt courageous, strong, happy and fulfilled but most of all, she recognised a self-love that wasn't there before.

Chapter 8

The Maiden in the Mirror

'I am beautiful, I am strong, I am fierce,' Parry repeated over and over as she trudged through the Cavern of Grey. She was wearing stone- coloured boots that reached her knees, grey stockings and a long- sleeved tunic to match. Parry didn't want to admit it but she secretly loved her outfit and with her stunning red mane, she looked like a schoolgirl gone bad.

'I am beautiful, I am strong, I am fierce…what the hell are those?'

Parry wrinkled her nose up at the Virgo symbols covering the cavern walls ♍.

It was cold, damp and smelled like her grandfather's attic. It made her wonder whether her family would even notice she was missing had time flowed the same on Bastion as it did on Earth.

'Ha! Dad would just think I was away at makeup camp or something.' Parry laughed out loud. 'Maybe my counterpart will be the sister I never had and treat me like an actual member of the family.'

She continued to stamp her way through the tunnel before reaching a cave very similar to the Mission Base but shrouded in white mist. In the centre sat a beautiful transparent throne constructed with grey glass and a gigantic mirror standing next to it. The mirror was decorated with white marble filigree doves and feathers. It was aesthetically pleasing and inviting. Parry practically skipped to the mirror and tucked the flyaway strands of hair behind her ears before stepping up to gaze at herself. What she saw reflected caused her to scream so loud she wouldn't have been surprised if the entire Mission Base had heard it.

The woman staring back was indeed Parry but decades older. Parry couldn't look away from her withered, sagging face. Her eyes had lost their green spark and now resembled a watered down version. Her face had lost its smooth, contoured planes. The skin literally hung off her bones, crumpled and pock-marked. Her hair was no longer a luscious red but a streaky white and liver spots nestled in the folds of her neck and sides of her face. Her expression was dull and bored, as if she were just waiting for death, no longer engaged in life. Her lips were chapped and slightly blue.

Regretfully, Parry opened her mouth and saw her beautifully straight white teeth completely missing from the hag's mouth. There was nothing but a gaping hole of ugliness. Parry gave a sob, staggering backwards. This couldn't be her future self. She had accepted getting old one day but to look this hideous and miserable? It just couldn't be! She was so glad Graham or any of the others weren't there to witness the worst moment of her life. She went to sit down in the throne and jumped when she saw a beautiful woman already seated and sneering at her with cold blue eyes.

The Virgo counterpart was without a doubt the most beautiful woman Parry had ever seen. She was wearing a grey silk dress that hugged her perfect, alabaster smooth figure. A string of pearls lined her swan-like neck and she wore grey silk gloves that looked similar to the ones Parry had worn at the Astrological Dance. Like Parry's, her hair was a deep crimson that tumbled in waves down her face and hung at the base of her lower back. Her lips were a blushing red and her eyes glinted like sapphires. Her delicate feet were encased in metallic heels. Parry felt threatened for the first time in her life. She was torn between admiration and pure envy. It was awful!

So this is what that word "insecure" feels like?

The Maiden gave a laugh which sounded a lot like the tinkle of a dainty bell.

'You thought you knew what beauty was until you looked in the mirror and compared yourself to me.'

'Great…I have an evil counterpart,' Parry grunted.

'I am not evil; I am merely superior to you in every way,' the Maiden said matter-of-factly.

Parry spun around looking for the exit but the shroud of white mist had intensified. Her line of sight was strictly limited to the Maiden and the mirror in front of her. It was like a typical dream scene in a movie with a nightmarish storyline. She turned back to find the throne empty once again.

'Where did you go? I need to speak with you!'

'Did you like what you saw in the mirror, girl?'

Parry couldn't see the Maiden but she could certainly hear her taunts.

'No! It was horrible and a gross misrepresentation of what I'm going to look like when I reach the senior years. I will age much more gracefully than that…like Helen Mirren.'

The mist began to swirl around the mirror and Parry saw the hag grinning devilishly at her again. In an instant, the face morphed back into the Maiden's. It pouted and then gave a sharp bark of laughter.

'I hate to break it to you, my dear but that is exactly how you are going to look when you are old.'

Parry defiantly plonked herself down onto the throne and enjoyed the look of disdain from the Maiden. She slumped sideways and stuck her boots in the air.

'I take excellent care of myself, dear Maiden. I brush and floss three times a day. I cleanse, tone, exfoliate, moisturise and use face masks. I exercise regularly and eat the healthiest food. I laugh and play and practise yoga. My hair has its own drawer of the most expensive and organic products. If that is me when I'm old then somewhere along my life I must become addicted to hard drugs.'

The Maiden smirked. 'Take your filthy boots off my throne and if you're going be seated at least do so like a lady.'

Parry wiggled her legs in the air and winked.

'I will be a lady when you show me a more realistic reflection of myself in that fancy pants mirror of yours.'

The Maiden huffed and disappeared from the mirror before materialising in front of Parry once more. She had the longest legs Parry had ever seen and they shone with silkiness.

'I cannot show you anything other than the truth. That is indeed your future if you continue to think so highly of yourself.'

'That's pretty rich coming from you,' Parry scoffed.

'I am pure perfection…I do not count. Do you know what a Maiden is, silly girl?'

'I really don't want to discuss your sex life right now or lack thereof.' Parry rolled her eyes.

'A Maiden is a woman that is pure...and not in the sexual sense but rather untouched by everything. I am untouched by time, stress, environment, influences and more. You, being a mere Earthling, are touched by all of these things and they will make their mark on you yet.'

Parry jumped up, her eyes burning with anger.

'Listen here! I am what men and women would call a goddess back on Earth. I have not been touched yet either and you know why? Because nobody is good enough for me!'

Parry bit her lip in shock. Suddenly, she realised what the Maiden had been trying to tell her.

'Nobody is good enough for me...'

The Maiden watched patiently. She walked over to the Mirror where the picture of the Parry hag was laughing wildly. Despite everything, it looked incredibly amusing coming from a toothless face.

'Parry, your beauty is quite literally what others would call a blessing and a curse. It is wonderful to be so beautiful but you keep everybody at arm's length due to your unreachable standards. The longer you make the external a priority, the quicker you will end up alone and frankly quite ugly.'

Parry thought back to how her Dad never paid attention to her and how much she resented him for it.

This whole time she had blamed him but in reality she had refused to show him anything real about her. When he had tried to discuss things with her she would laugh it off and ask for shoe money. At school she allowed all the boys in the yard to fawn over her but never bothered to learn any of their names. She had never been on a single date because nobody had measured up and it was hard for her to admit how lonely it was becoming. She suddenly felt lost. Looking up, she noticed the Maiden staring at her with the first kind look since Parry had entered the room.

'If I don't have my beauty...then what do I have? Who am I without everything?'

The Maiden waved her hand and the hag disappeared from the mirror. 'That is something you're going to have to find out, Parry.'

'Well, if I find that out will you promise me something?'

The Maiden looked apprehensive but nodded.

'Will you stop this war with the other counterparts and agree to all rule equally?'

With a small smile, the Maiden waved her hand again and the mist dispersed, illuminating the exit.

'When you come to me again, I want you to prove that beauty is not the most important thing. If you can show this to me, I will surrender the fight and convince my allies to do so as well.'

Parry looked longingly at the exit. She couldn't wait to see her actual reflection again. The Maiden cleared her throat.

'Right! I have to find something more important than beauty. Who are your allies?'

'I have two allied counterparts that will go to the ends of the universe for me.'

'And they are?'

'One is beast, the other man. They do not favour flame or water. That is all I will tell you.'

'Great, hopefully Danni knows what that means.'

The Maiden leaned in to kiss Parry's cheek.

'Thank you for coming to visit me. Believe it or not I understand why you desire beauty. All Virgos are pleasing to look at and are perfectionists. They take good care of their appearance and are meticulous when selecting lovers. All I ask is that you don't let the mirror rule your life.'

Parry nodded miserably at the Maiden and walked back through the dark tunnel until she could hear her group chattering. The smell of chilli was wafting through the entrance. Lunch had been served. Graham ran up to her wearing a burgundy beret with matching muscle tee and skinny jeans.

'How was it, darling? Was the Maiden divine or just diva?'

Parry smiled weakly. Ever since she had met Graham at Maltin's Tanning Salon a year ago, she had found a man who had met her every standard. She knew Graham felt the same way about her but due to their sexual preferences, they would only ever remain bosom buddies. In a way, their relationship was very similar to Hunter and Ambrite's except Hunter seemed to struggle with the fact that Ambrite was not interested in him romantically. Parry was quite happy to live with a gay man like Graham for the rest of her life. But there were things she would miss…

'She was divine but I realised a few hard truths about myself and now I'm feeling blue.'

Graham frowned. 'Blue means wrinkles, love, cheer up!'

Parry thought of the gnarled old hag and shuddered.

'What is it, darling? What did you learn?'

The Virgo felt an unexpected heat rise in her face before she completely snapped.

'There's more to life than just appearances! You may think the latest trends will keep you popular but really, who cares when you're just going to die alone!'

Graham stared at her with wide eyes and an open mouth.

She burst into tears at his expression. 'Just leave me alone,' she sobbed and ran to the showers. Stripping until she was completely bare, Parry let the stream of hot water nearly burn her skin as she cried and cried. It didn't matter how much she scrubbed, she felt unclean and for the first time in her life…ugly.

Chapter 9

Wisdom and Wine

Ronan watched Danni's mind tick over. He wanted nothing more than to lean over and kiss her. The secret was out...well to him anyway. He was in love and couldn't fight it any longer. He was waiting for the perfect time to tell her and now that Slade and Crawford were officially out of the way, he felt he had a fighting chance.

'One is beast, the other man and they do not favour flame or water...hmmm.' Danni twisted a tendril of hair between her fingers.

After Parry had briefly stopped crying in the showers, she had emerged looking like a puffy raccoon. The group and Graham especially had tried to get her to talk about what had happened but she had only shared the cryptic message given by the Maiden before returning to the bathrooms once more. Graham had tried to approach her but Ronan stopped him gently.

'Just let her be, man. When she's ready, she'll talk.'

Reilly had been kind enough to pull Ronan aside and tell him what the centaur had said about his counterpart.

'His weakness lies in his negativity hey?'

'That's what Chiron said but he also mentioned he was the most logical so maybe you can use that Capricorn intellect to win him over.' Reilly grinned.

The few that were still in the Mission Base crowded around Danni trying to work out the clue when she gave a yell that made Ronan jump.

'I've got it! She's talking about the elements! I can't believe it took me this long to figure it out! So if they don't favour flame or water then one is an Earth sign and the other is an Air sign. There are no beasts in the Gemini, Libra, Aquarius Mythology so that means the Air sign is man. It clearly isn't my Gemini twins as they don't know the meaning of allies so either Brodie or Slade will find out once they enter their Coloured Caverns. The Earth beast could either be the Taurus or the Capricorn. Ambrite has already gone through her Cavern so Ronan…?'

'Huh?'

'We need you to go through now and gauge whether your counterpart is allies with the Maiden. Can you do that?'

Ronan met eyes with Danni who was giving him an encouraging smile. She was so beautiful and he was completely distracted around her now.

So much for the cool, calm, collected Capricorn…

He wanted to tell her soon but was worried she would laugh in his face. Back on Earth, they had teamed up for the "Least Compatible Pair Challenge" which wasn't a good start. She had been so crazy about Crawford and Slade because they had suited her "astrologically" but in reality that had meant nothing. Would she give him a chance despite being on the other side of "The Wall"? The Wall was a theory Danni had created and told her group about in earlier meetings. Basically, the twelve signs were divided in half. All the Fire and Air signs lined up on one side of The Wall and all the Earth and Water signs lined up on the other. Dating within your side was preferable because you shared similar traits. If you wanted to cross the wall, you could…but the relationship had less of a chance to work out. Logical Ronan had personally found this ridiculous but he saw how much it meant to Danni and tried to factor in that it may count towards a humiliating and painful rejection. He felt a sharp jab in his chest whenever Danni squealed about Drew and Hannah not only being on the same side but sharing the same element. He was screwed.

Wow, if I continue this type of thinking, the negative Capricorn goat will welcome me with open arms!

Ronan strode toward the Cavern of Black, its gaping mouth dark and ominous. Danni stood next to him looking concerned.

'I'll be okay,' he reassured her.

She managed a weak smile and for just a second, her visible display of apprehension made him think he had a chance.

'I guess nothing could be worse than having a Gemini twin threaten to flatten your face with his foot.'

She laughed but Ronan couldn't join her. He was still torn between anger and fear at what could've been a disastrous outcome for the girl he cared so much about.

'From what Reilly told me, he sounds like a highly intelligent but incredibly mopey goat. I think I can handle it.'

'I know you can.' Danni smiled warmly.

To his surprise, she leaned in and folded her arms around his neck. He could smell the coconut oil from the showers around the ends of her hair and took the moment to breathe her in.

After what felt like more than just a casual friendly hug, she released her arms and stepped back. Ronan felt his face turning red.

'Errm…so time to find out if this goat has the goods! That doesn't sound right…'

Danni laughed and waved him towards the entrance of the cave.

He stepped through and immediately needed to duck due to the incredibly craggy, low ceiling. His shoulders began to ache as he continued to hunch over in order to avoid the roof that seemed to be getting smaller with every step he took. It was almost as if the passageway was made purely for the goat to move through and nobody else. He noticed the Capricorn symbols gleaming on the side walls ♑ and realised it was time to get on his hands and knees and begin crawling. Ronan had a mild tendency to claustrophobia. To him, it felt like the walls were closing in. It was becoming impossible to crawl any farther so he began to shift backwards only to bump into the back wall.

'Hey!' his muffled voice rang out. He was trapped and there was no room to move backwards or forwards.

Suddenly, a posh male voice sounded out of nowhere: 'Just relax. Embrace the element of Earth.'

With the assumption that the instructions came from his counterpart, Ronan closed his eyes and did his best to curl up into a comfortable foetal position. Visualising the grounding element of Earth, he inhaled and exhaled deeply. It was difficult ignoring the twist in his gut trying to remind him he was trapped in a cave and may never get out.

A gust of wind whipped through the cave and as Ronan opened his eyes, he felt himself falling through the bottom. The adrenalin pumped through his nervous system as he landed softly on a bouncy bed of grass. Jumping up, he shook out his stiff joints and took in his surroundings.

The cave was completely spherical, black and littered with stars. It felt like he was at a Planetarium or quite literally outer space! The floor was covered in soft grass with scraps of food, tin cans and rubbish scattered everywhere.

I guess goats all over the universe have the same appetites...

'I heard that!'

Ronan looked up to see a bed of rocks at the far north of the sphere. Sitting on the rocks was a tiny black goat with a scruffy beard, long vertical horns and a forest green mermaid's tail. It had a pair of spectacles perched on its nose and leered at Ronan with wide, crazy eyes. Ronan strode over to where it sat and tried not to laugh at the amusing sight before him.

'Find me funny do you, boy?'

Ronan did his best not to snort at the goat that ate tin cans but sounded like a butler named Jeeves.

'My name is not Jeeves it is Aegipan.'

'Quit reading my mind and body language, Aegipan,' said Ronan.

'My mother's name was Aega and my father's name was Pan hence the amalgamation.'

'That's very logical, Capricorn,' Ronan grinned.

Aegipan appeared pleased. He bleated and a chalice filled with red wine materialised on the rocks beside him.

'Please, Ronan, have some wine. Centuries ago, I became good friends with a man named Dionysus. As a gift for my loyalty, he gave me these chalices that never empty. This wine is direct from Ancient Athens…Sixth Century BC to be exact. It tastes the same now as it did all those years ago.'

'You were friends with Greek God Dionysus?' Ronan scratched his head. Aegipan nodded and flicked his mermaid tail in the direction of the chalice.

Ronan picked up the chalice and took a sip. It tasted like ancient history, passion, love, philosophy and literature. The velvety liquid ran down his throat and left him with a rich spice. It was the most amazing thing he had ever tasted. The chalice refilled itself and Ronan downed the second helping in a single gulp.

'Slow down there, Earthling! We have business to attend to,' Aegipan warned.

Ronan brushed his mouth with his sleeve. He felt much more confident and slightly lightheaded. Setting the chalice down, he cleared his throat.

'Yes, thank you for reminding me. So where do you want to start as you obviously know why I'm here?'

The counterpart sat up straighter with a look that meant business.

'When are you going to tell Danielle Hamilton you are in love with her?'

If Ronan had still been drinking the wine, this would've been the part where he spat it out in surprise.

'That's what you want to talk about? What about the fact you are at war with the other eleven counterparts? Ringing any bells?'

Aegipan snorted. 'Please...I already know that is a lost cause. My world and yours will surely end soon.'

Ronan could now see the negativity Chiron had mentioned to Reilly. The goat was downright pessimistic.

'I don't see it that way, Ronan,' Aegipan replied, reading his thoughts once again. 'I am the epitome of logic. Logically, I know the eleven other counterparts are stubborn and it is silly to presume that children such as yourselves will be able to save the universe from their egos.'

'So you have absolutely no hope that we can unite all of you?'

'None whatsoever but feel free to keep trying, I won't stand in your way and I mean that metaphorically not literally.'

Ronan felt so deflated he picked up the cup and drank more wine. Aegipan let him finish before speaking.

'Would you like to discuss professing your love for Danielle Hamilton now?'

Ronan laughed sadly.

'What's the point? The world is going to end anyway according to you.'

'Precisely! All the more reason for you to tell her while you still can. What do you have to lose?'

Ronan decided to try a different route.

'What do you think about the Virgin Maiden?'

Aegipan whooped. 'She is more pretentious than Hades itself!'

There goes that plan…

This meant the Taurean counterpart was loyal to the Maiden but Ambrite had already entered her Coloured Cavern before Danni could brief her.

Ronan tried to resist one more sip of liquid courage or he would end up telling Danni he loved her in a drunken slur. He held the chalice out to Aegipan who made it vanish with a blink of the eye.

'Do you think you should rule the zodiac?'

'Yes, but I have thought that since the dawn of time, Ronan. Milo's sly remarks had no influence on me.'

The goat shimmied off its rock and landed softly on the bed of grass beneath it. It began to slide on its belly around the patches of green, snatching up whatever scraps met its path. It was such a strange sight, Ronan could only stare.

Chewing on a rusted tin can, Aegipan looked like he was in heaven. He continued to chew until the can was uncomfortably lodged in his belly. To Ronan's amusement, he let out an alarmingly loud burp and bleated in satisfaction. Ronan knelt down next to Aegipan and ran a comforting hand over his belly. Aegipan closed his eyes in contentment.

The pair sat in silence for a few minutes. Aegipan appeared to have dozed off, full from his meal of ground scraps. Ronan continued to stroke his black hide. He relished the moment to plan his next move and hoped Aegipan wouldn't read his mind.

After a couple more minutes, Ronan gave a loud, deliberate cough. Aegipan opened his eyes and peered at Ronan through the tops of his glasses.

'Why should I tell her I love her? We both know she thinks Geminis and Capricorns are the worst match.'

'Because she may surprise you?'

'Ah! So you're saying I should base my decision on hope and faith rather than logic?'

Ronan grinned at Aegipan's look of defeat.

'I see…well I would rather be bested by a fellow Capricorn than any of the other signs.'

'Logic isn't always the way, Aegipan. I am a lot like you. Do you know what it was like to be a Capricorn and part of the Astro A Team? I used to think this stuff was a load of bull but Danni taught me another side to life. A life filled with mystery and that not everything has to be explained logically and scientifically. That's why I love her. She helped my father come out of his garage and start living again. She showed me a different way of looking at things. I think we are incredibly compatible and I hope she feels the same when I tell her...'

The goat bleated in surprise. 'So you are going to tell her?'

'Yes,' Ronan gulped. 'I am if you promise to believe in me and the Astro A Team. The universe may not come to an end. We have a chance to unite everybody including you. You think because you're the most logical that you should rule but that is a very black and white way of looking at things. Life is not like that. You need a balance and that's why all of you should rule together.'

Aegipan appeared thoughtful. He slid on his belly back to the rocks and used his front hooves to pull himself up. Ronan followed, his heart beating at crazy speeds.

'I am not an aggressive counterpart, Ronan. I would never harm my fellow counterparts nor force my beliefs on them. Just because I believe I would make an excellent ruler does not mean I am rigid in thinking so. Let us make a deal. If you tell Danielle you love her and she reciprocates, I will believe in your cause wholeheartedly and not resist it.'

'Thank you, Aegipan.' Ronan reached out and shook hand to hoof.

'Can I assist you with anything else before I transport you out of the Cavern of Black?'

Ronan thought for a minute then snapped his fingers.

'Danni is having trouble getting through to Castor and Pollux. She was nearly stamped to death in their last encounter. What is their weakness?'

Aegipan flicked his tail up and down, thumping the rocks. Clearly he loved being asked for advice.

'Identical in appearance they may be but one is weaker than the other…'

Ronan opened his mouth to respond and felt a gust of wind whip around his shoulders. Before he could say goodbye, he found himself standing at the entrance of the Cavern with Danni still talking to the group in a corner. He walked towards her sticky with sweat. Was he really going to tell her? It was now integral to their mission. She turned as she heard him approach and flung her arms around him again. He hugged her back and took a moment to stroke her hair. She pulled away looking flushed.

'How did you go? Does he have an alliance with the Maiden?'

'No he doesn't…in fact he said she was as pretentious as Hades.'

Danni's face dropped. He immediately felt guilty.

'Ambrite has already gone through her Cavern. Damn! We will have to brief her when she gets out and she can form the alliance next time. So what happened?'

Ronan told her about the claustrophobic cave and how the Cavern looked. He touched on Aegipan's logical, negative demeanour without mentioning anything related to his feelings for her. He even informed her about the wine which he missed dearly already.

She listened with fascination and a shine to her eyes.

'Wow, he sounds so interesting! I wish I could visit all the counterparts, mine suck. How did you leave it?'

Ronan couldn't tell her now but he could prepare her for it subconsciously. His wise counterpart would be proud.

'Aegipan said he won't resist our attempts at unity if I can show him a time where hope and faith won out over logic.'

Danni furrowed her brow. 'That sounds complicated. It would be hard to show that to the King of Logic himself. If I think of something I'll let you know.'

Ronan laughed nervously. He was worried that when he did profess his love, she might feel obligated as a way of aiding their mission.

'Oh, one more thing…I asked him if he knew a way to beat Castor and Pollux at their own game.'

Danni appeared genuinely touched. 'Yes?'

'He said that one is weaker than the other.'

Danni sighed. 'That doesn't help much but I guess we can suss out the weakling next time.'

'You and Charlotte are definitely going to have to work together on this one.'

'I guess that means we need to be as close as they are.'

'That's why it's so important that you and Charlotte get it together. If both of you aren't united, they won't take you seriously.'

Danni gazed over at Charlotte who was draped all over Crawford without any shame and Ronan felt a twinge of jealousy. Did she still have feelings for him? Did she wish she was in Charlotte's place?

'The last time we were there Charlotte lasted two seconds before touching Castor and fainting. She says she loves Crawford but if Castor had asked her to be his Geminian wife she would've said yes in a heartbeat. I tried talking to her before about banding together but she told me the only thing we had in common was taste in men. The nerve of that bitch!'

Ronan took a deep breath. 'Do you still love Crawford?'

She turned to him, her face softening.

'No, of course not. I don't even love Slade. In fact I never loved Slade…he just made me feel better when I was rejected.'

Ronan felt a spark of hope.

'Well, they are both idiots in my opinion. Crawford more so as Slade didn't really do anything wrong.'

'And why do you think Slade is an idiot?' Danni teased playfully.

Is she flirting with me?

'Ummm…well because you're so…'

'DANNI!'

Ronan and Danni spun around to see Ambrite visibly enraged and walking right over to them. She stopped in front of Danni with a look that would make all the counterparts cower in fear.

'I was starting to forgive you but after what I just went through… I hate you all over again!'

Chapter 10

A Bully of a Bull

Ambrite was torn between many feelings and emotions. On one hand, Danni had proven to her and Hunter that she was a loyal, trustworthy friend when they had spilled their deepest, darkest secrets to her. On the other hand, Danni had also proven she had the ability to betray her own best friend by hooking up with the one guy that was off limits. She would've left the Astro A Team that night had Garth not shown up. When she heard that Danni was nearly killed by her counterparts, she felt sick to her stomach which meant she obviously still cared. Hunter basically followed her lead; whatever choice she made, he respected and supported. Ambrite couldn't tell if he was torn up too or just empathising.

She decided it was her turn to enter the Cavern of Green and face off against her counterpart but going in without Hunter backing her felt slightly unbearable. Ambrite gazed at her shaggy-haired soulmate and smiled. How she lived life before him was a great mystery. They were closer than close; like *Will & Grace* but reversed. They spent every waking moment together and had even discussed having a baby together one day, adopting the scientific approach rather than the traditional one. Hunter was her rock and they balanced one another out beautifully. She could tell he was in pain when Asterion had forbidden him to accompany her in the Cavern of Green.

'What if the counterpart starts talking about your family and your grandfather and your…suicide attempt?' Hunter whispered the last part.

'I know…but I need to be strong and face this on my own just as you will have to with yours.'

Now they were standing by her bed as she picked out an outfit that didn't make her look like a weed. She rummaged through her closet and finally settled on a green pinafore with ripped stockings and matching long-sleeved top. She refused to remove her piercings or hide any tattoos. This was the real her and the counterpart had to deal with it.

'You look cute,' Hunter grinned.

Ambrite stuck out her tongue and made a rude gesture with her finger.

She noticed Reilly and Drew walking laps around the cave comparing closets. Crawford and Charlotte were in a huff over something as usual and Ronan, Graham and Danni were laughing over at the buffet table. Parry had already left. She had a very similar relationship with Graham albeit a bit more superficial but there was one glaringly obvious difference. Graham was not in love with Parry.

Ambrite knew how Hunter really felt but chose to ignore it. She just figured it would go away when he found a girlfriend or realised Ambrite wasn't just going through a phase. There were moments when the two of them were so close, cuddled up in bed and gazing into each other's eyes that she thought…maybe? But when she pictured being physically intimate with him it made her uncomfortable. He wasn't female and she just couldn't take it that step further. Ambrite had had girlfriends in the past but they never seemed to last long. They always wanted her to open up and she hadn't been able to do that with anybody except Hunter. They had all ended up leaving her with the same parting words: 'you need to let somebody in. Amb'. Why couldn't Hunter be a girl? She let him in without any reservations. Ambrite was still struggling with emotional intimacy. It was easy with Hunter. He had been through similar pain and heartache. She didn't need her parents to approve of him but one day, if she ever found true love, she hoped they would approve then.

Smoothing her hair, she turned to Hunter and smiled weakly.

'Well…I guess this is it?'

He placed his hand on the small of her back and led her over to the entrance. Despite the firecracker Hunter was when they had first met, he had definitely cooled down and become a real gentleman. He was going to make some girl very lucky one day.

'Whatever happens in there, don't buy in, Amb. They are going to use your weak points against you, I can just feel it.'

Ambrite nodded. 'I can feel it too.'

He cupped her face with his hands and kissed her softly on the mouth.

Startled, Ambrite froze and allowed their lips to connect without pressing back. When Hunter pulled away, he looked hurt. She felt the guilt weighing her down.

'Hunter...you know that I'm...'

'I know,' he cut in. 'I just thought with our closeness and all...'

Ambrite felt on the verge of tears. Why couldn't things just stay the way they were? Why did feelings have to come into it?

'Hunter, you're my best friend and my soulmate but that's all. Isn't that enough?'

'It is for now, but what happens when you find a girlfriend and I have to watch you? When you find somebody...you won't have time for me anymore.'

She opened her mouth but no words came out. What could she say? She couldn't deny it. A relationship would change everything.

Reaching forward with her hand, she stroked his cheek lovingly and strode into the cave. She could still feel his eyes boring into the back of her as she disappeared into the darkness.

*

Everywhere she turned, the Taurean symbol ♉ flashed bright green. She felt an itch on her ankle as if the tattoo was conversing with the marking on the wall. Ambrite looked down at her forest green combat boots and noticed she was standing in a pile of what she hoped was mud. The smell of freshly mown grass and bales of dry hay wafted past her nose. Sure enough, as she rounded the corner, a bright sunny field filled with unlimited acres of land came into view. The sun warm on her back made her happy. The landscape was so picturesque with rolling hills in the background and the clearest blue sky. A quaint red barn with a thatched roof was to the left and to the right, rows upon rows of wheat stood tall. Ambrite was about to examine the barn when she heard a grunt. Directly opposite her, a dark green bull the size of a car was staring right at her with menacing eyes. She froze.

It seemed like an eternity of eye contact before the bull began to slide its giant hoof back and forth, ready to charge. Ambrite yelped and without thinking ran directly into the wheat field. She could hear the bull roar and the clop of its hooves along the earth as it chased her into the golden labyrinth of grain. She didn't stop to look around. Weaving through the wheat, Ambrite ran for what felt like ten minutes. Stopping to catch her breath, she noticed the air around her was now relatively quiet. The bull must've lost track of her. She noticed a small opening to the right and stepped through, only to find herself exactly where she started with the now sealed up cave entrance behind her. The bull was trotting up and down the field snorting with laughter. Ambrite felt a surge of anger, her fiery stubborn attitude kicking back into gear.

'What the hell! Do you get your kicks scaring girls?'

The bull looked up and this time she noticed its beautiful bronzed horns. It shook its head, the brass reflecting in the sun. She heard a deep booming voice but the counterpart's mouth never moved.

'The field is an illusion. Isn't it clever? A lovely lady and dear friend came up with the idea. You could run for hours and still wind up here.'

'Yeah, freaking genius,' Ambrite drawled. 'Are you going to kill me or not?'

'Where would be the fun in that? I would rather see you squirm, Amber.'

Ambrite went bright red. Her hands began to shake.

'Don't call me that…ever!'

Ambrite had been christened Amber by her parents but she had always felt the name didn't suit the true individual she really was. Amber sounded like a snotty-nosed cheerleader that loved boys, parties and shopping. Ambrite was sex, drugs, rock and roll. The name signified self-expression and a free spirit. It was the person her parents didn't understand and didn't bother to get to know. Not that long ago, she had revealed to Danni that she had tried to take her own life due to feeling lonely and neglected by her mother and father. Hunter had shown her she could get love and attention elsewhere but all she had ever wanted was for her family to really see and accept her. They had never been interested in any part of her life and even refused to listen when she came out.

'Amber, it's a phase just like your hair and your attitude.' Her mother frowned before shooing her away and talking business into her mobile phone.

The Astro A Team had made Ambrite feel accepted and loved for who she was. In that moment, she softened towards Danni and felt that maybe it was time to forgive her.

The bull snorted once again which snapped Ambrite out of her reverie.

'I wouldn't forgive Danni so quickly if I were you. Did you know she told the rest of your group about your secret? Oh yes the one you confided to her...everybody knows.'

Ambrite stared in shock. Surely this bull was lying? It was trying to throw her off her game.

'You're lying...you just don't want to help me because you believe you should rule the stars.'

'You can believe what you like but she has proven herself untrustworthy with her closest friend so why should you be any different?'

The bull sidled up to a large apple tree that seemed to materialise from nowhere and bumped its carriage against the trunk. Several rosy apples fell from the boughs and littered the floor. One impaled itself on the bull's horn and the creature huffed dramatically. With caution, Ambrite walked over and beckoned for it to lower its head. Up close, the bull's hide was silky smooth. She badly wanted to touch it. Tentatively, it lowered down and she plucked the apple off the horn and extended it to him. Eyeing her suspiciously, its large leathery tongue rolled out and nabbed the apple in one gulp. She took a few steps backwards and picked one of the stray apples off the floor. The bull widened its eyes. Ambrite felt rebellious. The red fruit gleamed as she triumphantly sank her teeth into the peel. It dissolved and all that remained was the juicy flesh. She gave a contented, exaggerated sigh. The bull didn't lose its temper but merely nodded in approval.

'Danni taught me that Taureans love three things: food, nature and family,' Ambrite said. 'I can see that your Coloured Cavern has two of those things but you seem quite lonely.'

'I am not lonely. I told you I have a friend who helped set up my wheat maze.'

'Whatever you need to tell yourself to get by *Bully*!'

'My name is Cerus and I'm not interested in your opinion. Your leader is a typical Gemini, gossipy and likes the sound of her own voice. She told your secret to everybody. They pity you.'

Ambrite began to wonder if it was true. After her confession, she had noticed how much nicer everybody had been to her. What if Danni had told the group to treat Ambrite with kid gloves? Like a charity case? She still couldn't believe Danni had kissed her best friend's crush. She had betrayed her own best friend. There was no loyalty in Danni.

Cerus looked triumphant and clip-clopped around the apple tree. Ambrite was stubborn and held a grudge. She was certain now that Danni had spilled her secret.

'Okay, so let's say she blabbed, what does that have to do with you? Why do you think you should rule?'

'I guard the Tree of Life. What bigger responsibility could one have?'

Ambrite stared at the half-eaten apple in her hand and dropped it. She spat out the remaining juice in her mouth.

'It's too late…you already ate from it. I would've stopped you but Taureans are so stubborn.'

Ambrite felt sick. Her palms became moist and her heart rate sped up.

'What does this mean? What have you done to me?'

'If you eat from the Tree of Life you become immortal. You can never die and it's irreversible.'

Ambrite clutched her stomach and doubled over in fear. Tears pricked her eyes. So many people in this life would kill for immortality but she didn't want it.

'Does this mean I'm going to watch everybody around me grow old and die? How am I supposed to have a normal life?'

'You won't.' Cerus tilted its horns matter-of-factly.

Ambrite began to cry. When would she wake from this horrible nightmare?

'Do you see now why I should rule? The Tree of Life was trusted to me and every hundred years it bears these red apples. In that time, I am allowed to grant immortality to whoever I choose and I chose you, Ambrite.'

'Why?' Ambrite choked.

'Because you tried to take your own life and therefore you must be punished. Life is so precious. So your parents don't give you enough attention. Is that a good enough reason to end it all? You took it for granted and now it's all you have.'

Ambrite stood up and with tears blurring her face, she ran for the cave which was no longer sealed. She sobbed all the way until she reached the entrance and could hear voices talking. How long had she been gone? Time moved so slowly here. Wiping her eyes, she sat against the cave wall and regained her breath. This was all Danni's fault. She'd brought her here. She'd told her secret. She'd ruined her life and now it would never end...

*

Ambrite stood in front of Danni and Ronan trembling with rage.

'You...ruined...my...life.'

Danni's eyes were wide in shock. She took a step towards Ambrite who immediately stepped back.

'Ambrite...what happened? What did I do? Please tell me. You can trust me.'

'Ha!' Ambrite spat. 'Trust you? You told everybody my secret, didn't you? About my parents and my suicide attempt?'

Danni shook her head. Ambrite felt panicked when she noticed Ronan looking confused and horrified at the same time.

'You didn't tell anybody...did you?'

'What kind of a friend do you think I am, Ambrite? You told me that in confidence.'

The remaining Astro A Team members had begun crowding around the two of them, including Hunter who grabbed Ambrite's hand. Charlotte snorted and everybody turned to look at her.

'She's the kind of friend that kisses someone else's man!'

'Coming from you that's rich,' snarled Danni.

Ronan turned to Ambrite. She noticed he was so much gentler since he had joined the group. Was he in love with Danni? It certainly seemed that way.

'What did the counterpart say to you? It obviously tried to turn you against Danni knowing you were already having trouble trusting her.'

Ambrite suddenly felt ashamed. She had let Cerus manipulate her. She probably wasn't even immortal. It was all a big hoax to make her hate Danni and throw them off the mission.

'He told me that Danni had told everybody my secret back home.'

Hunter groaned. 'I knew I should've come in with you! It did exactly what I thought it would and used your past as a weapon.'

'Ambrite, I never told a soul about your secret, I swear,' Danni pleaded. 'I get that I'm not the most trustworthy person right now but I would never blurt out something that personal. You have to believe me.'

Ambrite shook Hunter's hand free and turned to Reilly.

'Do you trust her because I certainly don't?'

Reilly shifted uncomfortably. Drew and Hannah put their arms around her. Danni hung her head in misery. Slade took that moment to turn and run into his Coloured Cavern with Brodie yelling after him.

'I…actually saw what happened with Slade and Danni that day,' Reilly muttered.

'What?' Danni looked up.

'After my horrible encounter with Chiron, Garth came and comforted me. His dragon necklace has powers. It showed me exactly what happened that day. I saw Danni's resistance to Slade and how crappy she felt after the kiss…'

For the first time since that night back on Earth, Reilly walked over to Danni and grabbed her hand. Danni burst into tears and Reilly followed suit. They held each other and cried. Drew whooped with joy and Ronan clapped Hunter on the back grinning. Hannah also began to wail and joined in the big group hug.

Ambrite stood and watched the two best friends reunite. She felt terrible. Danni was trustworthy after all. She felt a tap on her shoulder and noticed Garth standing behind her.

'Come with me,' he whispered.

She took his hand and they suddenly reappeared in a private chamber. It looked similar to the Mission Base except ten times larger with an aquarium running around the entire sphere of the room. Ambrite noticed two attractive mermaids floating by and winking at Garth. He blushed and pulled her towards a throne in the centre where Asterion was sitting and looking very grave. Garth flopped down next to him and they exchanged worried glances.

'What?'

'We're so sorry Ambrite.' Asterion shook his head sadly.

Ambrite felt a familiar tightening in her chest. She let out a loud sob.

'It's true isn't it?'

Garth nodded sadly.

'We couldn't stop you in time. Once you took a bite of the apple, there was nothing we could do.'

Tears spilled down her cheeks. Garth reached out and took her hand again.

'What does this mean? Do I tell the others?'

'No,' said Asterion. 'We will explain it to them in due time. It is unfortunately irreversible. '

'This can't be happening...' Ambrite stared at the seaweed floating in the aquarium. Eternal life and nobody to share it with.

'We will give you two options, Ambrite. Should you succeed in your mission, you are welcome to live here in Bastion or you can return home. If you decide to return home however, you will need to find a way to keep your secret. You won't be able to stay in one place for long or form lasting relationships. At least here...you will be accepted.'

Ambrite suddenly felt like the loneliest person in the universe.

'Is everybody on Bastion immortal?'

Garth chuckled.

'No, but it isn't unusual here and time does move differently. Everybody knows that Asterion, myself and several others are. Cerus gives an apple to a person of his choosing every hundred years so there are a few floating around the town.'

'But if the counterparts never leave the caves then how would Cerus choose people?'

Asterion grimaced. 'They do leave the caves and appear in different guises despite our warnings. Some of them like to frequent Constellar now and then in disguise. Cerus in particular likes to take the form of a man and seduce who he pleases into eating an apple.'

Ambrite felt a familiar ire burn in her belly.

'Why didn't you tell us this? Especially me? You could've saved me!'

Asterion rose out of his chair and walked over to the aquarium where the mermaids giggled and pointed. He gave them a stern glance, shooing them with his hands. They pouted and floundered away.

'As I told you in the briefing, the counterparts…well some of them…are incredibly devious. They even fool Garth and me. We saw Milo leaving with an apple the day he visited and figured he was given one for sweet-talking Cerus. As it turns out, the apple was a fake. Cerus wanted us to believe he had given Milo immortality when really he was waiting for you.'

'Take me back,' Ambrite urged. 'I want to be with the others.'

Asterion sighed. He placed his hand on a shoulder. It felt so heavy.

'Think about what you want to do. You can stay in Bastion or go back home. It's your choice.'

Ambrite's watery eyes met Asterion's and she shook his hand free.

'It's not much of a choice…'

Chapter 11

Red Ram

One minute she was there and the next she was gone. Hunter began spinning in a circle like a dog chasing his tail.

'Dude, are you okay?' Drew raised his eyebrows. He looked pretty pleased that his two best friends were still hugging and crying.

'Have you seen Ambrite? I swear she was standing right next to me?'

'I'm sure she's just gone to the shower. Chill, man, it's not like she's your girlfriend.'

Hunter knew Drew was right but it didn't stop his desire to punch him. He still felt like an idiot for kissing her earlier. She looked so shocked. What was he thinking? As if she was interested in him that way?

He strode to the shower block and yelled her name. He was about to leave when he heard a whimper. Making his way to the source of the sound, he found Parry sitting on the tiled floor with makeup stained eyes and wet, stringy hair. It took him a moment to recognise her. She was usually so glamourous and put together. He kneeled down beside her.

'Are you okay?'

'We might as well get married,' she murmured.

'Huh?'

She slowly rose to her feet and wiped her nose on her arm in a very unladylike Parry fashion.

'My life is over so I might as well marry a rough, bad boy like you. I'll sit on the back of your motorbike and we can travel the world, never looking back. I won't have to care about my hair, my appearance, the latest fashions...'

'Umm okay...well I hate to disappoint you but I don't have a motorbike.'

Parry stared at him before bursting into another round of tears, walking back into the shower stall and slamming the door shut.

Hunter sighed deeply and walked out confused. He noticed Ambrite had returned looking very solemn. He ran over and pulled her into a hug. Once again, she froze and didn't reciprocate. He released her and held onto her shoulders. She refused to meet his gaze.

'Amb, where were you? What happened? Are you okay?'

'Hunter...I need you to leave me alone for a while. Please. Just let me think.'

He felt his heart rate increase. Something wasn't right.

'No, I'm not leaving until you tell me what happened and if we're okay.'

He reached out for her hand and she jumped back.

'Hunter, just go! Don't get close to me! This friendship has reached its use by date and we need to cool off.'

Ambrite's tone was harsh but her mouth had drooped. She was still looking everywhere but at him.

'Is this because I kissed you? I promise it won't ever happen again. We will go back to exactly as we were. Just talk to me!'

'We can't go back to how we were! Don't you see that everything has changed and...things are different now? Please, Hunter, just go. Go see your counterpart...please.'

Hunter began to walk away when he felt what Danni called "Rage of the Ram" kick in. He turned back and took hold of Ambrite's chin so she had to make eye contact. He could see the fear and sadness in her eyes.

'I thought we had the type of friendship that people dream about but apparently I was wrong. You're such a coward you can't even tell me what is going on much less look me in the eye. Well you know what...I'm done! You're too much of a mess anyway! Good luck finding another guy as devoted as me!'

Fuming, he marched into the Cavern of Red which glowed with such intensity it resembled the entrance to Hell.

'Hunter!' Ambrite called weakly.

Hunter didn't look back. He ran through the darkness guided by the flashing crimson signs of Aries ♈ to light his way. The tunnel was structured in one straight line without any twists or turns. It felt so good to feel the sweat drip down his back as he raced to an unknown place. Maybe his counterpart would be cool and they could kick back and talk about how strange women were. Whatever lay beyond, he clearly wasn't wanted back at the Mission Base. With every step, he could feel the cave becoming hotter. With every step, a loud rumble reverberated through the walls. What if this was the entrance to Hell? Hunter was slick with perspiration and could barely breathe.

The tunnel had transformed into a sauna. Hunter ripped his red tank off, scrunched it into a ball and shoved it into the pocket of his crimson baggy shorts. He was about to pass out from the intense heat when the sound of a boulder rolling made him look up. It took him several seconds before registering that he was standing above a volcano. It reminded him of the video games he used to play where he had to manoeuvre his character around in order to avoid the lava and lose a life. The loud rumbling that he had heard earlier was the molten liquid gurgling beneath a rickety wooden bridge that was so long there was no visible end in sight.

'Great! This looks so safe!'

Hunter walked to the beginning of the bridge and made the mistake of looking down. He wasn't afraid of heights but if the bridge broke, he wouldn't exactly land in refreshing cold water. He debated whether he should race across the bridge or crawl slowly over it. In every movie, the bridge always broke at the last second due to someone's extra weight. He opted for the turtle pace option. Kneeling on his hands and knees, Hunter looked forward and began to crawl. The rickety bridge swayed underneath, forcing him to shut his eyes and quell the nausea. The wood was so old he yelped as a splinter entered his finger. There was no time to backtrack or try and pull it out. Around the halfway mark, a bubble of lava burst and a drop flew up into his bellybutton. Hunter roared in agony, pawing at the planks in exhaustion. He could just make out a grey stone slab in the distance. There was actually an end in sight!

A devilish bleat caused Hunter to freeze. Shakily rising to his feet, he looked behind him and made out two blurry horns nudging at the rope that held the bridge together. The bridge suddenly dropped a metre and he yelled. The terrifying sound of thread beginning to snap was the catalyst for adrenaline. In a moment of sheer panic, Hunter began to race to the other end of the bridge, his feet banging against the boards. Just like an action film, he was about to reach the stone slab when the entire bridge gave way. Hunter bent his knees and sprang forward with his arms outstretched. Grabbing the edge of the slab, he hoisted himself onto the surface and lay flat on his back gasping for breath.

A sniggering 'baa' made him jump to his feet. A large ram the shade of blood stood in front of what appeared to be a wide stone cot with a wicked grin. The only part of the beast that wasn't red were the two giant ivory horns that curled above its head looking incredibly sharp.

Hunter pulled out the sweaty tank top from his shorts and wiped his dripping face. He flung it at the ram and smirked when it hooked onto its left horn.

'That's what you get for nearly killing me!'

The ram laughed with an open mouth full of sharp teeth. It looked positively terrifying.

'What's wrong, Hunter?' the ram boomed. It trotted up and down the slab. 'Girl troubles?'

The counterpart was trying to bait him and it was working. Hunter had purposely run through the Cavern of Red to escape his issues with Ambrite and it was still being flung in his face.

'Don't act like you know me! You don't and you certainly don't know her!'

The ram laughed again. It was infuriating.

'It is *you* that doesn't know her. She is hiding something from you, something big. Perhaps you should ask her what happened when she faced off against Cerus.'

Hunter assumed Cerus was the Taurean counterpart.

'I did and she wouldn't tell anything except that everything has changed. What happened to her? Tell me!'

'I can't and I won't. Let's talk about you and who you were before Ambrite. Have you dealt with the wreckage your father left behind? Did your therapy help you?'

Hunter's blood boiled hotter than the lava pit beneath his feet.

'That is none of your business! I don't answer to you!'

The ram stopped trotting and stared at Hunter pointedly.

'Well that's hardly fair. You've come into my home demanding answers from me. How about we play a game? Every time you answer a question honestly, I will give you an answer in return. If you lie, you will have to have to take a step across the bridge and keep in mind...I know when someone is lying.'

Hunter spun and saw the bridge was back but looking more rickety than ever.

'Deal! I'm in hell already, might as well make a game of it.'

'That's the spirit!' The ram winked and clopped over to the bridge.

Hunter followed and stared into the deep orange and yellow pit of liquid. His head swam and he had to hold onto the post to steady himself.

'Question number one,' the ram trilled. 'Do you wish Ambrite was mortal and in love with you?'

'I don't see how that…' Hunter started and stopped when the ram made the bridge wobble. 'I don't know what mortal has to do with anything but yes of course I do. I love her. I want us to be together. Enough honesty for you?'

He nodded energetically. He was clearly enjoying his sick game of Truth or Burn.

'Now a question for you. What is your name?'

'Ares, which I share with the Greek God of War. Really? This is your question? My name is hardly relevant but oh well. Question number two: if Ambrite chose to live on Bastion permanently would you stay with her or go home? Think about it!'

Hunter felt a sudden pang in his stomach. What was Ares alluding to? Surely Asterion and Garth wouldn't allow that?

'I…yes if she chose to I wouldn't leave her side.'

'Are you sure about that? She will never love you romantically. You would spend your life on another planet with a girl that will always be just your friend when you could go back home and find somebody that will reciprocate your feelings.'

'Yes! I wouldn't abandon her on this planet! I don't just want her in my life for romantic reasons.'

Ares shook his woolly head. 'You are lying…step onto the bridge please.'

Hunter was about to protest when he remembered how attracted he had been to Ambrite from the beginning. He had never really seen her as a friend. Their friendship was just a stepping stone to deeper love for him and even though he knew she was gay, he had always hoped to be the exception.

Stepping forward, he placed his toe gingerly onto the decaying wooden board and finally his entire foot. The contact produced a loud creak causing Hunter to tightly shut his eyelids. After a moment of minor swaying, he opened them to see the ram grinning at him.

'Because you lied, I now get to ask you the next question and you have to wait a turn. If you lie to me again, you take two steps.'

Hunter took a deep breath. 'Okay…bring it on.'

'Why did you really join the Astro A Team? For such a long time you rebuffed Danielle's invitations.'

Hunter felt guilty every time he remembered hanging up on Danni or yelling at her after his sessions with Dr Yates. It wasn't until he met Ambrite and spoke to her after the session that he began to feel better about himself. The afternoon they had spent together left him feeling hopeful about the future. After that, he had taken Danni up on the offer to start his life over.

'Don't you know the answers to these questions already? Why waste time playing this game?'

'I want to know if I can trust you. You will get nowhere with me if you lie.'

'Okay, I joined because I wanted to start my life over and figured the first step to doing that is to make friends.'

'And because Ambrite was going to join?'

'Well that helped!'

'Good answer! Your turn.'

'Can I get off this bridge? Lie and move forward? Tell the truth and step back?'

Ares snorted. 'You will stay right where you are. You cannot get off the bridge until I say the game is over no matter how many truths you tell.'

Hunter took a second to think about his question. It was so hot he could barely concentrate. He longed for the cool stone Mission Base and a hug from his best friend.

'Okay, why do you believe you should rule the stars?'

The ram's next answer shocked him.

'I don't.'

'But...I thought you were all fighting over the same thing.'

'Not all of us.'

'Why don't you feel like the rest of them?'

'Ah I don't think so! One question at a time! My turn. Do you take after your father?'

Hunter felt sick to his stomach. Flashes of walking into his parents' bedroom that day filled his head. He couldn't shake the lifeless look on his father's face draped over the bed with a needle in his arm. It was without a doubt the most traumatic moment of his life. His mother had cried while her son had vomited violently in the garden. It had felt like a purging of his soul. She had left his father after that. It wasn't the violence towards her that made the decision; it was seeing Hunter fall apart.

He wiped the hot, wet angry tears from his eyes.

'I am nothing like him…'

'Lies!'

'I'm not!' Hunter cried. 'He was violent and abusive towards my mother! He was a drug addict and a gambler! How do I take after him?'

'Hunter…you are such an angry person. You've come a long way since joining the Astro A Team but deep inside you resides a dark swirling vortex of anger that you haven't dealt with. Your father has the exact same temper. When your mother didn't give him what he wanted, he saw red. When Ambrite didn't return your feelings, you yelled and ran here. She does not have to love you back. She does not owe you something that is not within her. Of course you are not evil nor cruel like your father but your anger has the ability to lead you down a similar path if you don't take a hold of it.'

Hunter stood rooted to the bridge. He wasn't scared of the lava beneath him, just numb. Ares nodded to the bridge behind him and Hunter took two steps back. He didn't know what to say. Nobody, not even Dr Yates, had ripped him apart like that before. A desperation tugged inside him. He would do anything to not be like his father.

Ares looked slightly guilty. Hunter made a gesture for him to ask his next question.

'The reason I am not in this war is because despite being named after the word itself, I do not condone it.'

'That's not a question,' Hunter croaked.

'No, it's an answer. You wanted to know why I don't feel like the rest of them and I am answering you. I have struggled a lot with my own temper and this is exactly the type of situation I needed to avoid. It's a silly argument. The Greek Gods had their domains to rule. Hades oversaw Hell. Poseidon the Sea. Artemis the Moon and so on. My domain is Aries. I rule a section of the stars and that is all.'

Hunter nodded. He was still in shock from his epiphany.

'If you answer the next question honestly, I will allow you to ask one more of me and then you may leave for today.'

A sudden creak in the bridge made his heart jump. He planned to answer the next question with every ounce of truthfulness in him just to save his own life.

'If Ambrite chose to live on Bastion permanently, would you stay with her or go home?' Ares repeated.

Hunter met the cool, calculating eyes of the ram.

'I would go home. I want to get married and have a family someday. I love Ambrite but if I stay, I will give up any chance of that and probably end up resenting her.'

Ares nodded. Suddenly, the left side of the bridge snapped and Hunter found himself clinging to the frayed rope on the right. The rope burned his clammy palms. He looked up at Ares in despair.

'Quick! Ask your question and make it count!' The ram shouted.

Hunter was focusing all of his attention on not letting go and surviving. He had to think fast. With one last hoist, he pulled himself up further on the rope and clutched tightly with clasped hands.

'How can we unite all of the counterparts?'

A cool mist began to swirl around Hunter. He struggled to hear as Ares began to fade.

'You cannot unite us. There is a traitor in...'

That was all Hunter managed to gather before he was forced to let go of the rope. Expecting to burn up in the lava, Hunter was elated to find himself transported swiftly by the mist back to the cave entrance. Despite his new understanding, he was still suffering from a broken heart...

149

Chapter 12

Repairing the Urn

Slade had fled without even thinking. He was tired of the love triangle drama he had ultimately created between Reilly and Danni. If he had known it was going to cause this many problems, he wouldn't have bothered in the first place. He thought he had loved Danni but looking back, maybe it was just a strong crush. Whatever the case, the cat-fight that had come after had well and truly put him off relationships for good. He had heard Brodie call after him and felt guilty. They usually did everything together but she couldn't understand how lonely he had felt after Danni had stopped kissing him that day on the couch.

Was he a bad guy? He had wrestled with the question every single day. It was driving him mad. At least he looked better than Crawford. He had never liked the slimy guy and even less so now that he was seeing Charlotte who was downright loathsome. The pair deserved one another in his opinion. He raced down the narrow cave lined with symbols he presumed were for Aquarians ♒ until he found himself in another cave with three potential pathways. One to the left, centre and the right. There was absolutely no indication on the cave walls which path was the correct one. It took him a good five minutes of contemplation before he walked down the middle entrance. His reasoning for this was simple.

Aquarius dominated the month of February. February was the second month of the year ergo the middle cave was the second entrance from the left. He wasn't sure about the other options but the middle cave was pitch black and drafty. The wind whipped around his aqua pair of jeans and matching jumper. As he walked forward, the resistance of the wind became harder and harder to move against. He wondered whether to turn back and choose a different direction. One session back at Bouquet Reserve floated through his mind.

'Aquarius may seem like a water sign as the symbol represents a water bearer but those squiggly lines are actually air waves being caught in a vessel. Just like my sign Gemini, Aquarians and Librans favour the element Air and are brilliant communicators,' Danni moved her hands in a wavy motion.

Slade hadn't given her lecture much thought until now. If Aquarius dominated the element Air, perhaps he *was* in the right tunnel. He braced himself and pushed his body forward, countering the gusts that were intensifying with every step. He could hear a faint muttering in the distance that travelled along the air waves. It sounded a lot like 'oh no' being repeated over and over. The gales were now so strong Slade's eyes began to water. He closed them and reached with extended hands to feel his way. Terrified that his hands would soon make contact with a giant fan, Slade lowered his arms and took a large step towards the incessant cries.

'STOP!'

Slade's eyes sprang open and he found himself no longer in a tunnel but what appeared to be the top of a castle turret. It was a stone circular room with a window ledge overlooking the sea. Gulls squawked in the distance as the sun was beginning to set. Slade looked down to see bronze shards littered all over the floor and his raised foot about to step on one. A handsome but visibly stressed man with golden curly hair stood in the centre with his palm facing Slade.

'Do not take another step! I have to repair my urn and if you smash any of the pieces it will take me even longer to put it back together.'

Slade quickly moved to a clear corner. He slid his shoes off as an extra precaution.

'Is this why I was nearly blown over back there? Did you release this wind?'

He noticed the man had the clearest blue eyes. It was like looking through a glass bottom boat. He wore an aqua toga and was grasping the handle of the broken bronze urn for dear life.

'Yes. I released the Aquarian Air and if I don't repair this urn, it will never return to its rightful home. '

'What powers does Aquarian Air have? Why is it so important to keep it contained?'

The counterpart frowned. He placed the handle on a wooden stool and knelt down with his head in his hands.

'They have the ability to send a person or even a group of people to anywhere they wish. You just have to step outside this balcony, jump and ride the air current.'

'Oh! Like a portal? We had a pond back home that sent us here to Bastion.'

'A portal is not the same as Aquarian Air,' the man murmured.

He picked up a large shard and placed it next to the handle on the stool.

'How so?'

Slade knelt down and felt his head throb at the impossible task before him.

'Aquarian Air doesn't teleport, it gives you the full experience of travel. If you wanted to visit a planet that was five days away, you would ride for that amount of time. You would eat, sleep and whatever else...'

Slade raised his eyebrows. A portal seemed like the obvious choice in his opinion. Not only would he get to his destination instantly, he wouldn't have to poop off an air wave.

'I know it may not seem as efficient as a portal,' the man read his mind. 'But it actually is. Not only do you get to experience the power of flight but the air wave will be loyal to you. It will be available whenever you need it. A portal is temperamental and doesn't always reappear, plus it requires a strong amount of magic to conjure.'

'How does one obtain Aquarian Air?' Slade mimicked the conversational style of his counterpart.

The man finally made eye contact with Slade and laughed. It wasn't a cheerful laugh but rather one of deep condescension.

'Nobody obtains it because it belongs to me. I allowed Asterion access decades ago when he required safe passage through the universe to a planet seven weeks away. It was an emergency and I trust that man but otherwise it remains in my urn… until now.'

Slade glanced at the bronze debris before him. It didn't seem like anybody would gain access to the Aquarian Air again. A plan began to formulate in his mind.

'What can I call you?'

'Ganymede.'

Slade vaguely remembered the name coming up during the Astrological Mythology session at Bouquet Reserve.

'Like Jupiter's planet?'

He nodded. 'I discovered the planet long before yours did.'

'Wow then you're really ol...wise?' Slade backtracked but not before Ganymede frowned.

'I have lived a very long time, yes.'

The counterpart really didn't give him much. He figured close-ended questions would get him nowhere.

'So if you've lived for thousands and thousands of years as a guardian of the Aquarian Air and your urn is now broken...what is your purpose?'

To his surprise, Ganymede broke down, giving a high-pitched squeal.

'I don't know! This is all I've ever known and if Asterion learns that I broke the urn...he will probably find a replacement counterpart.'

Slade was horrified. He hadn't expected Ganymede to become a weeping mess.

'How did the urn break? After all this time are you honestly telling me it has never broken before?'

'Never!' Ganymede continued to wail. 'I was admiring the view from outside this window. The urn was resting on the altar and all of a sudden, I heard this woman scream. I jumped, knocked the altar and watched it break before my eyes.'

Slade furrowed his brows. The scream could've come from Parry. She had looked incredibly distraught after her visit. However, Ambrite had screamed at Danni in anger for thinking she had divulged her secret to the group.

'I know this sounds weird but what kind of scream was it?'

'Terror. The woman was clearly in shock at something she saw or heard.'

'Parry.' Slade murmured aloud. 'I'm not sure what she saw but when she left the Cavern of Grey, she was beyond terrified.'

Ganymede's ears pricked up and he boyishly wiped his eyes on his sleeve.

'Did you say Cavern of Grey? The Maiden is wondrous. She and I have a special bond...'

Suddenly, Parry's advice jogged Slade's memory.

'One is beast, the other man. They do not favour flame or water.'

Ambrite's counterpart had been the beast but she had already left before Danni could inform her. The man was clearly Ganymede and he favoured air as his element not water or fire. Parry had explained that with the allegiance of the Maiden's two allies, she would in turn help Parry unite the stars.

'Listen, my friend Parry who you heard scream...well she made a deal with the Maiden. The Maiden said she would help Parry with our mission if she was able to locate her two allies and gain their allegiance. Are you with us?'

Ganymede let out a snort so loud, it would've caused the urn to shatter if it hadn't already.

'No, you listen to me. If it wasn't for your friend, my urn wouldn't have broken in the first place. She caused all of this trouble and now you're asking me to help you? There is nothing I wouldn't do for the Maiden but I need to see some justice before I do what you ask.'

'Sure. What do you need?'

Ganymede drew himself up and puffed his chest.

'This Parry will have her voice box permanently removed!'

'Umm...how about I just help you fix the urn instead?' Slade suggested.

'Deal.' Ganymede exhaled and returned to his normal height.

Slade spent the next hour on his hands and knees picking up pieces, sighing loudly and knocking heads with Ganymede. The process was incredibly frustrating. Ganymede swore that when two correct pieces connected, they would magically fuse together without needing any glue. There had been no evidence of this so far and Slade began to wonder if the group were worried about him. He knew Brodie would be at the very least. They worked together in silence until Ganymede stood and walked to the window overlooking the glittering sea.

'Do you think the Maiden will ever love me?'

'Huh?' Slade looked up and saw Ganymede staring at him with pathetic, puppy-dog eyes.

'Do you think the Maiden will ever see me as more than an ally? I have loved her for centuries. She refuses to join with anyone. Apparently the word Maiden translates to alone for eternity.'

Slade was about to tell him to stop being such a pansy when he remembered feeling a similar longing for Danni. They had been so close to starting a relationship but at the last moment he was banished to the friend-zone for Reilly.

'I spent a long time hoping Danni would want to be with me. At first I thought Crawford was the obstacle but after him it became about Reilly. As much as the rejection killed me, I had to accept that Danni just didn't want to be with me. I was the bandage to her broken heart and that was it.'

'How did you come to this place of acceptance?' Ganymede took a step closer.

'It sounds lame but I realised my own self-worth. At the end of the day, I want someone to want to be with me. If a girl has to question and doubt then don't I deserve better than that? Don't I deserve a girlfriend who knows from the start that I'm the only one she wants?'

'May I be so bold?' Ganymede lifted a finger.

Slade gestured for him to speak freely.

'Wasn't Reilly in the same position as you? She also wanted your love and you didn't reciprocate. Isn't that what you humans call a "love triangle"?'

Slade felt the familiar pangs of guilt associated with the night of the Astrological Dance. Reilly confessing how she felt. Him staring at her blankly. The realisation dawning across her face before she ran away crying. He too had rejected somebody who had genuine feelings for him.

All of a sudden, two pieces of the urn that Slade had been fiddling with fused together accompanied by a whirring sound.

'Hey!'

Slade beamed up at Ganymede, holding the joined bronze shards.

His counterpart scurried over and they began connecting piece after piece with a renewed confidence and interest. It didn't take them long until only the handle on the stool was left. Ganymede picked it up and offered it to Slade.

'Please…do the honours.'

Slade held his breath and pressed the handle against the belly of the urn. It whirred and stuck fast. The urn shimmered and gleamed. It was now perfectly smooth and devoid of any cracks.

'Yes!' Ganymede cradled the urn lovingly. He walked to the entrance of the cavern, held the base against his chest with the opening facing the windy tunnel. Slade heard a rumbling and closed his eyes as a full force of wind burst into the room and swirled around them. The sound was deafening and his hands were numb from the icy gales. He feared being blown out of the open window.

'Slade! Open your eyes!'

He opened them to see Ganymede clutching the urn tightly. The hole worked as a vacuum, sucking and pulling on the resisting invisible element. He held onto Ganymede's robe as they drew the mischievous air closer to them. Transparent fingers grasped the entrance tightly but the power of the magic won out and with a final inhalation, the urn captured the Aquarian Air once more.

Ganymede rested the urn on the altar and gave Slade a triumphant grin.

'Thank you for helping me, Slade. As promised, I will align myself with the Maiden and your cause. I do believe I would make an excellent ruler of the stars but after today…well I've learnt that protecting the Aquarian Air is quite a task in itself.'

Slade nodded. 'It's an important job. The universe needs you to keep it up.'

Ganymede flushed. He walked to the cavern entrance and with a wave, it illuminated the path back to the Mission Base.

'Go forth, Slade. Return when the time comes. Perhaps the Maiden will favour me for helping you out but if she doesn't, I am happy to wait for someone who will.'

Slade reached out and shook Ganymede's hand. He looked at the polished urn and smiled.

'I know what it feels like now to be rejected and do the rejecting. I am never going to put myself in that situation again but it's nice to know that even after all the drama…some things can be repaired.'

Chapter 13

The Balance between Good and Evil

Brodie kept throwing glances at the Cavern of Aqua where her brother had fled nearly thirty minutes ago. They had always been close but since the blow up between Danni and Reilly, he was so quiet and sullen. He didn't want to talk about it which was difficult for someone like Brodie who spent so much time trying to keep the peace. Brodie started to wonder if her diplomatic nature was doing more harm than good. After all, if it hadn't been for her, Charlotte would never have met Danni. Danni's heart wouldn't have been broken by Crawford. Slade and Danni wouldn't have hooked up and Reilly's friendship with her would have remained intact.

Brodie sucked in a breath. That long chain of tumultuous events was a heavy burden to carry but she still felt responsible. By nature, Brodie considered herself to be pretty quiet and a pushover so as not to rock the boat. Slade was the only person who understood her. He used to comfort her by calling her easy-going but the reality was, she had been walked over her whole life. Brodie had thought she was doing the right thing by inviting Charlotte to Bouquet Reserve and it had resulted in drama, tears and fall-outs. Despite being in the same cheerleading squad, the minute Charlotte had hooked up with Crawford, she had barely spoken to Brodie at all. Even on another planet with nowhere to run, there was no friendship between them. Brodie considered getting another tattoo that read "Door-Mat" across her forehead. She felt foolish and embarrassed. What purpose did she serve in the Astro A Team? Garth had said they were all connected and here for a reason but she was starting to think they had picked the wrong Libran. Her counterpart awaited and it terrified her. What if she was told she didn't belong in the Astro A Team? She honestly believed Garth and Asterion would realise any day now that she was the black sheep and be sent home. She pictured Asterion's booming voice banishing her back to Earth.

'Brodie, you've done nothing but cause trouble since day one. You call yourself a Libran?'

Danni had told Brodie that Librans were incredibly beautiful people. They represented harmony, balance, kindness and peace. So far, her only contribution to the group had disrupted friendships and caused tension.

She heard giggles and smiled warmly at Danni and Reilly sitting on the bed hugging and talking animatedly.

They looked so deliriously happy at being reunited. Drew and Hannah were locked in a warm embrace near the aquarium. When those two were together, the rest of the world didn't exist. Parry and Ambrite were nowhere to be seen. They had both been visibly upset after leaving their Coloured Caverns. Hunter and Slade had already left to face their counterparts. Ronan and Graham were sipping juice by the buffet and laughing. Charlotte and Crawford were arguing as usual in a corner. Everything seemed as it should be. Order had been restored but for how long?

She walked over to the closet and pulled a blue hoodie over her tank top. Hoisting up her loose jeans, Brodie picked up a brush and ran it through her silvery blonde hair. At least she had been lucky in the colour department. Her outfit looked like something she would actually wear on a weekend. Brodie waved to Danni and Reilly who gave her a thumbs-up. Her bedroom and the entrance to the Cavern of Blue was closest to the shower stalls. Brodie paused as she heard a sniffing sound coming from the cubicles. She was about to investigate when she felt a tap on her shoulder. Spinning around, she saw Charlotte standing in front of her looking tear-stained and flushed with frustration.

'Crawford and I had another fight,' she whimpered.

Brodie shuffled her feet. She felt her face turning red. It was that same nervous and uncomfortable feeling that came with saying "no" to somebody.

'Uhhh, I'm about to see my counterpart. Can it wait?'

'I thought you were supposed to be my friend,' Charlotte sniffed.

Brodie gave a particularly loud laugh. A few members of the A Team looked up. She noticed Crawford was now lying on his bed with his back to everybody else.

'Friend? You have barely spoken one word to me ever since you and Crawford got together. All you do is fight! Perhaps it's time to call it quits?'

She instantly felt terrible. It was so unlike her to confront anybody let alone a spoilt brat like Charlotte.

'Charlotte, I'm sorry. I didn't mean that.'

To her surprise, Charlotte didn't explode. She just shrugged.

'Maybe you're right. Maybe I only wanted him because Danni had him first. He's become so needy and it's dragging me down. Thanks for the chat.'

With that, she turned on her heel and bounced over to the buffet.

Brodie shook her head in disbelief. Charlotte hadn't even acknowledged the first part of what she had said. She only cared about how Crawford no longer served a purpose. She truly was a horrible person. How she and Danni were ever supposed to unite was beyond comprehension. Crawford was also an idiot for being sucked in. He knew what a mistake he'd made letting

Danni go. Now he had to sit there and watch her relationship with Ronan blossom. It was pretty obvious those two had chemistry.

Brodie decided not to hesitate a moment longer. Maybe she was the odd one out but it was time to earn her keep. She took five steps into the Cavern of Blue and screamed as she fell through a black hole, landing on a gigantic slide. The slide was large enough to accommodate at least ten people comfortably and it spiralled downwards into a dark abyss. Brodie would've been terrified if the experience hadn't been unbelievably fun. She whooped and cheered as the momentum picked up speed. Her cheeks hurt from smiling. The walls were bright blue and covered with Libran symbols flashing in neon colours ♎. It reminded her of the amusement park at Santa Monica beach back home in the States. Her family would spend their summers by the pier rollerblading, surfing and slurping on their traditional mint choc-chip ice creams. A sharp pang of homesickness jabbed at her heart. The slide felt bottomless. It kept going and going leaving Brodie no choice but to clasp her hands behind her head and let gravity take the wheel.

After about twenty minutes, the slide stopped snaking and dipped straight down. Brodie held onto the side which was a bad idea. The plastic rubbed against her skin making her cry out in pain. Her butt ached from the hard surface beneath her and she was feeling slightly nauseous. The slide decided it was finally bored of its passenger and Brodie found herself flying through the air. She braced herself for a sticky end before landing on a soft, blue chaise lounge. Heaving a sigh of relief, she stretched herself out on the couch. The motion of the slide still ran through her body like the feeling after stepping off a treadmill or travelator. She closed her eyes, allowing her dizzy spell to fade. The scent of lavender drifted past her nose. It was calming. She inhaled deeply, her lungs filling with floral fumes.

Brodie opened her eyes and sat up to take in her surroundings. She was in the most picturesque garden. Rows upon rows of brightly coloured tulips, roses and orchids lined the walls of the blue cave. A fountain in the centre trickled quietly with shimmering golden water. Trees with bright red, orange and yellow foliage gathered around the lounge. Bushes with sprigs of violet lavender swayed in the artificial breeze. There was no sign of the slide she was on before nor any visible entrance or exit. It didn't matter. She was in paradise and nothing could make her want to leave, not even her counterpart. Brodie and the others had been very curious about what shape or form the Libran counterpart would take. It was the only symbol in the zodiac that was not a human or creature. She had joked earlier that she would probably be conversing with a giant pair of scales but now she was wondering if that was true.

Before she could guess, the sound of dragging made her heart stop. She jumped off the lounge, ducked and peeked around the right leg. In the distance, she could see something grey scraping along the path. It was difficult to make out but the sound and shape of the figure was something out of a horror movie not a garden oasis. Was her counterpart a deformed stone gargoyle? It moaned in extreme discomfort. Brodie's kind nature forced her to bite the bullet and help the creature. She stood and walked slowly towards the figure that had reached the fountain. To her surprise, the mystery person was an old woman made of stone. Her entire body was tilted to the left forcing her hand to drag along the floor as she shuffled. Her right hand was stuck in the air. If she had been a human, her bones would've broken and the muscles torn. Either way, it made Brodie squirm just looking at her. She ran to the left and attempted to lift the old woman who stared straight ahead expressionlessly. Beads of sweat formed as she pushed and pulled, doing her best to straighten the woman up but no amount of force could budge the heavy hand.

'It's no use,' the woman rasped. Her unblinking stone gaze did not meet Brodie's eyes.

'What do you mean? How do I get you upright?'

'You cannot…'

Brodie stopped trying. She walked over to the fountain and splashed her perspiring face with refreshing water. The old woman didn't move. Brodie knelt in front of her lopsided head and waved. Nothing.

'I don't mean to be rude but are you blind?'

'I have no use for sight,' the statue replied. She noticed the woman's mouth didn't move but the words were clear enough.

Brodie looked around at the lush greenery. It seemed like a cruel joke to live somewhere so beautiful and not be able to witness it.

'Why can't I help you?'

'Because you cannot tamper with magic as ancient as the universe itself.'

'I don't understand…is magic keeping you this way or were you born deformed?'

The old woman gave a gravelly chuckle. It made Brodie wince.

'I am not deformed. I am out of balance.'

'Oh…'

Brodie finally grasped what was in front of her. The old woman *was* the scales. The imbalance of the stars fighting was keeping her weighed to one side. Only once they united would she be able to stand upright.

'I gather from your exclamation that you understand my predicament?'

'Yes. You need the fighting to stop and restore balance.'

The birds chirped somewhere in the distance. The Cavern of Blue was such a place of peace yet the Libran counterpart was a representation of the corruption on Bastion. This was why they were here. Even though none of them had seen the counterparts visibly fighting, there was tension among them all. They were like stubborn children having a tantrum. If this animosity and stubbornness persisted, they would stop working together and the universe would be in great peril. Asterion and Garth had made out that they all thought they deserved to rule but the old woman just wanted to stand up straight.

'It's more than that my child. There is something wrong here in Bastion, I can feel it…'

The wind whipped through the trees. Brodie shivered. The words had sounded so ominous.

'Do you have a name?'

'Equas meaning equality,' the counterpart rumbled. 'I represent justice, temperance and righteousness.'

Brodie trailed her fingers in the golden water. Could it be starlight?

'When did you start to fall out of balance?'

'It began when that representative from Cassius arrived.'

'That makes sense.' Brodie nodded. 'Milo was the one that told all the counterparts they should rule which caused all of you to start fighting in the first place.'

'He never came to visit me. I have heard from some of my allies that he spread these falsehoods among the others but nobody aside from you has entered my Cavern in quite some time.'

'That's odd…why wouldn't he visit you?'

'Because I represent the balance between good and evil. His intentions were fuelled by evil, greed, jealousy and malice. I would never have acknowledged his claims and therefore he did not bother with me.'

Brodie couldn't wait to discuss the other counterparts with her group. Which ones were resistant to Milo's words and which ones had taken him seriously? Were they all manipulative like Garth suggested? Hers certainly wasn't. Equas played such an important role in Bastion. It was a shame she suffered so physically when things weren't level. There wasn't much more to discuss with her counterpart. All they could do was try to bring peace and harmony to the stars.

'Equas, is there any way I can help align the signs that have been influenced by Milo's words?'

The old woman began to move again. She began by pressing her left stone hand into the ground and using it as a lever to push her slanted body forwards. The right hand remained in the air, strong and straight. Her feet shuffled one at a time. It was a slow and grinding process.

'You can do one thing for me, child.'

'Please tell me.' Brodie walked in front of Equas. Her eyes stared straight ahead. It was no longer eerie but comforting. The old woman may have been blind but she saw the bigger picture and that was what mattered.

'You can cease doubting whether you belong here. Librans may not have dominant natures but we are leaders nevertheless.'

'I have never considered myself a leader.' Brodie flushed. Back amongst her friends, her suggestions had always been met with a 'nah' and eventually she'd given up voicing her opinion.

'I don't mean a leader that is boisterous and always speaks their mind. I refer to those that lead by example. They don't need to say anything. Their morals, virtues and good hearts are infectious to those around them. A true leader inspires others to follow. They do not demand or buy respect. It is earned and I see this potential in you.'

Brodie was glad Equas couldn't see her trembling lip and watery eyes. In just a few words, she had said everything Brodie had ever needed to hear. Danni had done a good job making her feel special but nobody had ever believed in her before. Not even Slade. She was in the right place and it was time to re-establish balance among the stars.

'Thank you,' she whispered. 'What can I do in the meantime? Asterion said our mission could take months and months but you didn't need any convincing at all.

Would you like me to come and visit you while the others work with their counterparts?'

'You do not need to visit although I will never decline the company. I have been trying to tell Asterion for months that something is terribly wrong here on Bastion but he refuses to listen. Perhaps if it comes from you he will finally take notice?'

'What is wrong? What do you know?'

'I sense an uprising. Something or someone here means to do us all harm. This is all I can tell you. Time is running out...'

Chapter 14

The King of the Jungle

How had things come to this? He had always been the charming, handsome guy, the life of the party. In less than a year, he had ruined relationships, friendships and was now stuck with a bratty girlfriend who kept picking fights with him. Crawford was ashamed to admit he was a little bit shallow. His group of friends had always been the type to stick with the girls that were stunning but fake rather than form quality relationships with girls like Danni who were real and pretty. Now he was kicking himself.

Ronan and Danni seemed to be growing closer which was great but the longer he stayed with Charlotte, the more he wanted to throw himself off a cliff. The only time she was any fun was when she wanted something. The rest of the time, she was moody, rude and pretentious. He couldn't even define their latest argument. Reilly and Danni had made up. Crawford had told her he was happy for them both and Charlotte had blown up, accusing him of having feelings for her enemy. He then reminded her of being seduced by the Gemini counterpart and she had burst into tears. It was these ridiculous, petty fights that made him question his own sanity.

Deep down, Crawford knew Charlotte didn't really care about him and vice-versa. He was weak and gave into the slightest temptation from her. Recalling the Astrological Dance made him cringe. He had been all set to meet Danni and have a dance with her, maybe even make it official. Charlotte had shown up right on time wearing barely anything and had thrown herself at him. He couldn't resist the type of girl he had always gone for. The cheerleading blondes had this way of turning him into a drooling zombie.

It was no excuse and he had broken the trust of a really innocent girl. In turn, broken-hearted Danni had kissed Slade and hurt her friendship with Reilly. The whole thing had become a massive mess. He had tried making amends with Danni but when it was pretty clear she would never be romantically interested in him again, his low self-esteem had led him right back to Charlotte who loved using their relationship as a weapon against his former flame. He had made a firm decision that once or if they ever returned home, he would break up with Charlotte. It would be way too difficult and chaotic were he to do it on Bastion. The Astro A Team had become so much more than a group of teenagers hanging out. They were a family experiencing a unique mission that nobody else would ever understand. It was important that Crawford's "family" liked his girlfriend and not one of them did. He didn't even like her anymore. He noticed her skulking around the buffet table, glaring at everybody and shoving her face with peanut butter cupcakes. Their eyes met and she scowled fiercely. He shook his head and stood up.

It was time to meet his counterpart and get it over with. Crawford was embarrassed to admit how terrified he was to enter the Cavern of Gold. Not only did he anticipate coming face to face with a terrifying lion but he knew it would use every bit of ammunition against him. It was "Judgement Day" for Crawford and he wasn't likely to leave unscathed. After the incompatibility challenge, he and Drew had unexpectedly bonded. He could tell during their macho game of basketball that Drew had wanted to hate him for hurting his best friend but by the end, they were slapping each other's backs and watching crazy cat videos on YouTube together.

As he stood outside the entrance, he was grateful to see Drew giving him an encouraging thumbs up. Crawford smiled weakly. He wished he was back in Bouquet Reserve raking leaves. This pastime had always been a form of meditation for him. Crawford didn't give Charlotte a second glance as he stepped into the mouth of the cave. As soon as he entered, the entire cavern was thrown into darkness.

Suddenly, the atmosphere began to heat up and Crawford found himself in the middle of a green, lush jungle. The air was thick, dense and humid. He could hear monkeys screeching, wild boars grunting and elephants trumpeting. He could smell hot, tropical rain one would only find in a thriving, abundant rainforest. Crawford could feel his gold cargo shorts and t-shirt beginning to stick to him. All of his senses were on overdrive. He couldn't believe how alive and beautiful the artificial setting was before him. It made him sad. If human beings hadn't contributed to so much environmental destruction, the entire planet would have flourishing rainforests exactly like this one.

Despite hearing a constant cacophony of animal sounds, no actual creatures emerged or made themselves physically present. Crawford began to relax. It seemed he was safe. He heard the sound of rushing water in the distance and ran through the thick greenery until he emerged in the middle of a vast lake with a towering waterfall. He was overwhelmed by the natural beauty surrounding him. Without a care in the world, Crawford slipped off his sticky t-shirt, shorts, socks and shoes before diving into the crystal blue water. It was the perfect temperature. Crawford swam towards the waterfall and submerged himself underneath to reach the hidden cave beyond. Surfacing behind the fluid curtain, he stepped onto the slippery black rocks.

His heart stopped when he suddenly noticed a large crocodile waiting in the pool below. How could he have been so stupid as to throw himself into a body of water without scanning for deadly reptiles first? The crocodile snapped its jaws together, its eyes alive with bloodlust. Crawford yelped and ran into the cave for protection. It was pitch dark, moist and craggy. He didn't dare go forward for fear of getting lost or worse. The cool atmosphere made him long for the clothes he had so recklessly stripped off and a sharp pebble under his foot made him cry out in pain. He jumped up and down, cursing his foolishness. This was not going well…

The cherry on top of the cake came in the form of a resounding, bellowing roar. Crawford had stumbled into the lair of his mighty counterpart wearing nothing but his underwear and hopping on one leg. Whimpering, he scanned the darkness for his worst nightmare. Why did he have to be born a Leo? The roars had ceased but faintly he heard low, threatening growls.

'Who is there? Show yourself!' Crawford's voice trembled.

The growling increased as did the soft padding of paws. There was nowhere to run or hide. Land *and* water enemies lay in wait. A flicker of orange caught his eye before he found himself flat on his back with heavy paws pressing down on his chest. Crawford emitted a less than manly scream. A gigantic male lion was staring into his eyes, its breath hot against his face. Crawford took one look at its glinting, sharp teeth and squeezed his eyes shut. The lion continued to growl and lift one paw and then the other, applying pressure on his muscular chest.

'Please don't kill me! I am the Leo representative from Earth!' Crawford spluttered, his eyes still closed.

This was the end. Crawford turned his head to the side. He didn't want to witness the finishing blow. Instead, the lion leapt off Crawford's chest and sat by the entrance of the waterfall. With a screwed up face, Crawford opened one eye, then the other and sat up in amazement. His chest hurt but he didn't care. He was alive and not kitty chow. Still shaking, Crawford stood, using the cave wall for support.

'Why didn't you kill me? Not that I'm complaining!'

The lion growled in warning. It was his way of saying, 'I haven't...yet.'

A large buzzing insect came into the cave and flew dangerously close to the lion's face. It began batting its paw at the pesky bug. Crawford took that moment of distraction to slip out of the cave. He surveyed the water below and saw it was clear. The crocodile must've become bored and left. He could see the green bank in the distance with his clothes still lying in a pile. He could make it in time if he took a running leap. Crawford ran to the edge. The cool mist of the waterfall sprinkled his arms and legs.

He was about to dive headfirst when he heard a commanding voice behind him.

'You really are a coward, Crawford.'

Crawford turned to see a teenage boy with a shock of orange hair and wearing dirty rags. The boy was a head taller than Crawford but he looked fifteen years old. His face was perfectly smooth and unblemished except for the dirt marks on his nose. He had coal black eyes that held no emotion in them. Crawford felt like he was staring into the eyes of a demon.

'Who are you? Where did the lion go?' Crawford darted his head around.

'My name is Leonis,' the boy stated monotonously. 'That was my animal form. The Crab, Goat, Ram, Bull, Scorpion and I all have human forms as well. This gives us the opportunity to blend in with Bastion society.'

Crawford knew Hannah, Ronan and Ambrite had only seen their counterparts in animal form. He wasn't sure what Hunter had seen and Graham hadn't gone into his Coloured Cavern yet.

'What do you like to do in Bastion?'

Leonis frowned. 'Please don't waste my time. I would like to focus on the fact you are a giant coward.'

Crawford scoffed. He didn't have to put up with this. He turned to jump again and noticed to his dismay that the crocodile was back. Leonis sported a wicked grin.

Defeated, Crawford sat on a flat mossy rock. He longed for the showers back at the Mission Base.

'Can I at least have my clothes back?' he muttered.

Leonis nodded and Crawford found himself back in his t-shirt, shorts, socks and shoes. They were perfectly dry and laundered.

'There is no reason we cannot conduct this conversation without your dignity intact,' Leonis said.

'You know, for a pubescent boy you sure do talk like a grown up.'

'I may look like a child but I am not one. I have been around for thousands of centuries. Have you always been a coward?'

Crawford let out a giant sigh. 'Why do you keep calling me that?'

Leonis laughed. 'Where do I begin? You broke Danielle's heart. You are courting Charlotte despite disliking her immensely and instead of dealing with me, you chose to run.'

Crawford opened his mouth to protest before slumping forward. He *was* a massive coward. He hadn't been honest with Danni. He was intimidated by Charlotte and his contribution to this all-important, life-saving mission was to flee. Why did he do that? The more he learnt about his character, the more he wanted nothing to do with it.

'You are a disgrace to the Leo constellation.' Leonis paced up and down much like his animal form. His wild orange mane and calculating manner added to the likeness.

'Leos are generous, kind and above all, brave. If you wish to receive any sort of assistance from me, you will have to redeem yourself with a great act of bravery first.'

The disgraced Leo stood up in despair. 'Like what? Do you want me to dive into the pool with the crocodile waiting for me? I'll do it! I'll break up with Charlotte. I'll apologise over and over to Danni, just tell me what to do!'

Leonis strode to the edge of the cliff and snapped his fingers. The crocodile nodded and swam off. Leonis gestured for Crawford to jump into the danger free body of water.

'You are free to go Crawford. I told you I will not deal with such a coward until you redeem yourself. A great act of bravery is not breaking up with somebody, it is acting selflessly without expectation.'

'Wait!' Crawford pleaded. 'Please give some guidance. I don't want to be a coward anymore. I want to like myself again.'

He was embarrassed to feel tears running down his face. He was sure Leonis would call him a coward again for crying. Instead, the teenage boy patted his arm.

'You've just taken the first step, Crawford. You will know what to do when the challenge presents itself. Come find me when you like yourself again.'

With that, Leonis morphed back into a lion. It gave a less contemptuous growl and padded back into the dark cave. Crawford felt helpless and humiliated. He leapt into the pool and swam back to the shore. Following the clear trail back to the Mission Base and without speaking to anybody, Crawford slumped back down on his bed and drew the covers over his head. One day he would be considered a brave man but today was not that day…

Chapter 15

The Sting of Seduction

Lucky last. It was all down to Graham. Had they really visited all of their counterparts in just one day? Logical Ronan had kept reminding them that time moved differently here. What seemed like a day in Bastion could be a week somewhere else. It was hard to tell seeing they hadn't seen the actual city outside. Was it day or night? Did the sun shine fiercely on this planet? Did birds sing in the trees? Were the people friendly or hostile? Graham was starting to think this was the only place on Bastion they would ever see. He was also remembering how close he had been to leaving the Astro A Team before winding up here and being caught up in a life or death mission. Back on Earth, Graham had felt like an outcast for being gay. He had been incredibly self-conscious and scared that he wouldn't be accepted for who he really was. It touched him every time he remembered how supportive everyone had been in the end but he still felt like an outsider looking in. There was nobody here that truly understood him.

Perhaps Ambrite? But even she was so close to Hunter he couldn't be sure if she was actually bisexual.

Parry was his idol and had been the second she had entered Maltin's Tanning Salon looking flawless and demanding a French manicure. He loved flipping through magazines with her, judging celebrities together and shopping for weekly new outfits whilst sipping on the latest juice cleanse. The only issue was, she wasn't a man and she wasn't overly deep. Graham was a romantic at heart. He wanted nothing more than to experience true love and be with a loving boyfriend who bought him flowers and listened to him talk for hours.

Danni had mentioned early on about Scorpios having a possessive and jealousy tendency in their relationships. He could see those traits coming through whenever he pictured his perfect man. He would never possess a partner exactly but he did want somebody to call his own. He didn't want anybody to come inside their relationship bubble and heaven forbid anybody should make eyes at his future beau! Graham was starting to become impatient that it would never happen and he certainly wasn't going to find love in an alternate universe. Not only that, his best friend was acting incredibly strange. She would not stop crying in the bathroom and refused to tell him what had happened. It had scared him senseless and put him off entering his own Coloured

Cavern. Now it was the end of the day and he was the only one left…

The rest of the Astro A Team had returned and they were all dying to share their experiences with one another but had decided to wait until Graham had had his own encounter. He was still dressed in his burgundy bell bottoms and tight shirt that outlined his sculpted torso. The colours were hideous but the man wearing them was pure perfection. Maybe his stylish skills alone would wow his counterpart? He highly doubted it. Feeling apprehensive, Graham turned to his friends who waved in encouragement. He was slightly hurt that Parry hadn't seen him off. How bad could it have been? She was acting incredibly selfish.

Making everybody laugh, he strutted dramatically into the dark cavern, letting out a whoop before everything went dark. The cavern glowed with the symbol ♏ just like the one on his ankle and everything shimmered mysteriously. The more steps he took, the brighter the walls became until he realised he was standing outside looking up at a blanket of beautiful stars. The air was hot and the ground was soft. Sand! He watched his burgundy loafers sink into the warm granules and a happy laugh escaped him. He was outside! He was no longer stuck in a claustrophobic, cold dark cave.

The desert stretched on endlessly under the perfect night sky. It was eerily quiet and devoid of life. Graham was finally at peace. He unbuttoned his shirt and lay it down on the sand. Lying down on his back, he clasped his hands behind his head and gazed at the wondrous twinkling lights above him. One day, he would do this with his partner and they could make up funny names of the stars together.

'Why, hello there...,' a smooth voice rang out.

Graham jumped up and pulled his shirt on. He spun around to see a breathtakingly handsome man with olive skin in a burgundy cape. The figure before him was tall and dark with gorgeous green eyes. His face was unshaven in a groomed kind of way and his teeth were whiter than the moon at midnight. Graham's heart began to beat in a manic rhythm. Surely this wasn't was his counterpart? And was he checking him out? The man before him seemed to be surveying Graham in a flirtatious manner.

'Hello!' Graham exclaimed a little too loudly.

The man walked over and extend his hand. When they connected in a shake, Graham swore he felt electricity spark between them. They lingered before releasing and stepping back.

'Graham, it is lovely to meet you. I am Serket which translates to scorpion in Ancient Egyptian. I believe you are here on an urgent mission?'

He spoke with such elegance and grace. Graham imagined them waltzing around their decadent mansion complete with butler, chef, shopper and dog-walker.

'Uhhh, yes we are here to unite the signs who are apparently at war with one another…does that ring any bells?'

Graham wanted to slap himself for sounding so stupid.

'I am aware that my brothers and sisters wish to rule Bastion because they believe themselves to be the most entitled.' Serket's eyes flashed.

'And you don't feel that way?'

'Oh no, I do. I am incredibly powerful, Graham…more than they all know.'

He looked so fierce that Graham took a wavering step back. In an instant, the look was gone and all that remained was his dazzlingly, seductive smile again.

'You are incredibly handsome for an Earthling. You must tell me your secret of youth.'

Graham flushed. 'Ahh well, my family owns a beauty salon so I get a lot of free treatments and I work out at least six times a week plus I eat clean.'

He was rambling like a crazy person. Serket continued to smile hypnotically.

'You also look fantastic. I mean do you have a gym here in the desert or just genetically good skin?'

Serket laughed. 'You are most entertaining, pretty one. I am immortal, which is, ironically, my secret to youth.'

A shiver went down Graham's spine at being called pretty. Could Serket be the one? The man he had been waiting for?

'What's immortality like? My best friend Parry, who's a girl by the way, wants eternal life as well. She even contacted some Romanian guy over the Internet hoping he had vampiric connections.'

He sounded like a gossipy teenager rather than the sophisticated adult he wanted Serket to see him as.

'I am not sure what vampiric is.' Serket screwed up his perfect nose. 'Immortality is a wonderful thing. There is so much potential and an entire galaxy to explore.'

'Asterion told us the counterparts remain here on Bastion and aren't even supposed to go into the city…is that true?'

Graham felt a cool wind circle his shoulders. The temperature in the desert appeared to be dropping at a rapid rate. He shivered and gasped when Serket appeared behind him. He took off his cape, revealing a burgundy fitted suit and draped it over Graham. Leaning in close, Serket whispered into his ear, 'What Asterion doesn't know won't hurt him…'

Their eyes met and Graham instantly closed his, hoping Serket took the opportunity to kiss him.

Instead, he felt Serket's hand take his. Graham cried as he felt a sharp jab in his palm before a strong wind began to rise from their feet, creating a mini dust storm. The stars above exploded and Graham found himself standing in the middle of a desolate wasteland full of craters. Did they just time travel? Where was Serket? What was this place? He took a step and heard a loud crunch under his foot. Looking down, he noticed unidentifiable charred bones and jumped in fright. His new man had a kinky side that was for sure!

'Do you love it, Graham?'

Serket walked towards him, glowing in his tailored suit and beaming from ear to ear.

'What is it? Whose bones are these?' Graham couldn't keep the hysteria out of his voice.

'Shhh, my pet, it's just a creature. Probably one that lived here for centuries before I found it.'

He could hear the sounds of scurrying. Sure enough, little black scorpions peeped out of the craters, their eyes red and menacing. He noticed a crumbling tower in the distance, its dilapidated façade in need of major construction.

Graham wanted to be back in the twilight desert where it was romantic and heading in a good direction.

'What is this place?'

'This is where I come when I need to be away. It also gives my little scorpions freedom to run around. I don't like rules, Graham. They restrict me. I don't like that old fool either with his dancing monkey in a top hat.'

Graham nearly laughed out loud at the accurate description of animated Garth.

'I want to build a new empire where I rule the stars and move away from Bastion with their regulations and disgusting Unsigned.'

The Unsigned were the civilians who did not know their sign. They were allowed to wear whatever colours they wished and were generally pitied by others. Garth was one of the Unsigned.

What Serket was confessing went completely against the mission but Graham was too in love to care.

'Join me, Graham.' Serket clasped his hand tightly. 'You can rule by my side and together we can start a new empire of Scorpios. Clearly, we are the most superior sign...full of power and leadership.'

Serket swayed seductively like a cobra about to strike. Graham nodded. It sounded like an excellent idea. This was his opportunity to spend eternity with a man who worshipped him. Something felt wrong but every time Graham searched his mind for what it was, he was overwhelmed by powerful images of them ruling side by side. They would be forever in love...forever young.

'What do you need from me?' he asked.

Serket dropped Graham's hand and took hold of his shoulders. He gazed hypnotically into Graham's eyes.

'When you return to your Mission Base, lie to your friends. Persuade them that you were incredibly successful with me and that I have promised to talk to the other counterparts about unifying. I don't care how you word it, just sound convincing. Then, ask them to let all of you celebrate at Constellar, the nightclub in Bastion. Once you have everybody in the club, meet me on the roof alone and we can return here. We will begin building our empire immediately, my love.'

Graham couldn't tear his gaze away from Serket's mysterious eyes.

'But won't they know I'm gone and realise what's happened?'

'By then it won't matter. I will have enacted my final part of the plan.'

Graham shook from elation and adrenaline. His new man was so intelligent and sexy.

'What's the plan?'

Serket pulled Graham in for a long, lingering kiss. As the kiss deepened, Graham felt like he was floating. He was so incredibly lucky. When they finally broke apart, he noticed Serket's face flushed with excitement.

'By tomorrow night, all of your friends and the Unsigned of Bastion will be locked in Constellar and massacred by my army of Scorpions...'

PART III
CONSTELLAR

Chapter 16

A Time to Celebrate

It was the end of an incredibly long, emotional and confronting day. The Astro A Team had pushed their beds together again, piled their plates with buffet food and were awaiting Asterion and Garth to arrive so they could brief them on all that had happened. Danni noticed the diversity of expressions on her friends' faces. Her best friend Reilly, Drew, Hannah, Ronan, Brodie and even Slade looked happy. On the other hand, Ambrite, Hunter, Crawford and Charlotte seemed miserable. What really blew Danni away was the extreme contrast between the bosom buddies Graham and Parry. The perfect Virgo looked absolutely devastated whilst the dashing Scorpio appeared almost euphoric. He kept bouncing up and down on the bed with excitement and a permanent blush to his cheeks.

'What the hell happened to you?' Ambrite spat bitterly.

'Let's just say my encounter went really, really, really well,' Graham giggled.

Ambrite made a sick sound and turned her back. Something seriously wrong had happened; even Hunter couldn't comfort her. He was weirdly keeping his distance and trying hard not to look over at her every couple of minutes.

Danni was hoping they would have a day off tomorrow. She needed some time to plan her next encounter with Charlotte. Castor and Pollux hated them even more than before they had arrived. They wouldn't be easy to engage with but thanks to Ronan, she knew to focus on the weakest of the pair. Danni couldn't deny the flutter in her chest whenever she thought of the Capricorn. She didn't want to admit how much she liked him out of fear but it was undeniably strong. After the week they spent together back home, Danni had felt a chemistry between them. It grew when he had stuck up for her at Bouquet Reserve and since they had arrived at Bastion, they'd "conveniently" always found things to talk about. There was just one problem. He was a Capricorn, which was her least compatible match. She felt silly but did the stars really lie?

Danni thought of her horrible counterparts and shook her head. Would she really give up love because of the way the planets were positioned? She glanced over at Ronan who gave her a warm smile. Her heart melted. She was ninety nine point nine per cent sure he felt the same way but of course there was always that small chance of rejection. Perhaps she would let him come to her this time. It seemed odd to be contemplating her love life in the middle of a dire mission on an alternate universe.

'Astro A Team,' Asterion's voice boomed from every corner of the cave. 'Please take your seats around the large throne in the centre of the room for a mission debriefing.'

The team rushed over to the throne with their plates of food and sat themselves in front of it. Shortly, the familiar golden light appeared, shimmering until Asterion had materialised in front of them once again. Garth simply popped into view and slumped into his smaller throne like a student in detention.

The Keeper of the Stars eagerly leaned forward, his hands clasped.

'Well…how did you all go?'

'Don't you already know? Weren't you watching us all?' Hunter grunted.

'We watched some of you, not all. Mainly we just monitored those of you we believed to be in actual physical danger.'

'What if we don't want to share what happened,' Parry croaked.

She looked like she'd still been crying. It was dark days when Parry Mason chose to wear grey tracksuit pants and a hoodie from her elaborate wardrobe.

Garth tut tutted at the emotional Virgo.

'I understand some of you have been through a lot but if you have anything that could help with our mission that would be very much appreciated.'

Nobody spoke except Graham who couldn't stop humming and smiling with his eyes closed. Danni had never seen him act this way.

'Ask him,' Crawford pointed. 'He's obviously had a good experience and wants to share.'

Asterion nodded. 'Graham, did you want to talk about your meeting? We are forbidden to inspect the Cavern of Maroon under the counterpart's orders. What was he like? He only ever appears in his large scorpion form which must have been terrifying at first?'

Graham frowned before bursting into laughter.

'I only ever saw Serket in human form and what a human! Oh we had the best time together and there is no need to hear anybody else's stories because he gave me fantastic news. He's going to talk to all the counterparts and persuade them to unite! We don't have to do anything else! We are all saved!'

The entire room was thrown into dead silence. The Astro A Team, Garth and Asterion merely stared at

Graham with their mouths open. After a minute passed, it was Charlotte who surprisingly spoke.

'Is this true, Graham? Can I really go home now and never come back?'

Danni snorted. *Trust Charlotte to think only of herself.*

'Oh yes, but I was thinking because of our success, we should all visit Constellar tomorrow night and celebrate! What do you think Asterion? Surely we deserve it after such an intense day?'

The wise Keeper looked uncharacteristically stunned.

'This is all so unexpected. I honestly thought I would need to keep you children here for months but after just one day you have managed a success of this magnitude? You most certainly are welcome to visit Constellar tomorrow evening!'

The group cheered except Ambrite who stood up suddenly and stamped her green combat boots.

'Hold on a second! We are not out of the woods yet. Just because Graham's counterpart said he would talk to the others doesn't mean they will agree and all partake in a big group hug. This hasn't changed anything!'

'Actually, sweetness, it has changed everything,' Garth beamed. 'The Scorpio counterpart has the power of persuasion and seduction. He is the one you want on your side.'

Danni felt a big sigh of relief. If Garth was correct, the Scorpio counterpart could change everything and she would never have to see those bratty twins again...or make nice with Charlotte.

'I don't get why the Scorpio counterpart couldn't have done this to begin with. Why need us when he is so influential?' Slade wondered.

Graham was still humming strangely. Asterion stood up and placed a hand on his shoulder.

'Well, that is clearly thanks to this bright young man here. He used his own powers of persuasion to convince his counterpart to work his. And the fact he showed himself to you in human form speaks volumes. We have never seen anything more than the scorpion itself. You truly are to be commended. You are, simply put, a hero, Graham Maltin.'

The Astro A Team began to applaud and cheer. Parry planted a big smooch on Graham's lips. Charlotte went to kiss Crawford who to Danni's amusement pushed her away. Reilly, Drew, Ronan and Hannah pulled her into a big group hug. It was so nice to be back to normal again. Brodie and Slade high-fived and Ambrite smiled weakly in Hunter's direction.

When the hubbub began to settle, Asterion and Garth sat down.

'Well, I believe it's safe to say we are all very pleased with the outcome of today and will certainly be celebrating tomorrow whilst our scorpion counterpart does his best to persuade the others. It is probably for the best that you have a break from them all and vice-versa. I understand some of you have had difficult times today. This was to be expected so try not to take any of it to heart. This is what they do but it doesn't mean it's true. In the afternoon, we will open the purple doors and you may explore Bastion before entering the club that evening. There are hair salons, beauty parlours, clothing shops and more if you decide to make an effort.'

All eyes turned to Parry, expecting her to be excited but she turned her face away, seemingly bored.

'Remember to wear your colours at all times,' Asterion continued. 'You will find many of the Unsigned within the town. Don't treat them like lepers as some of the others do. They are just like everybody else. Also, some of the counterparts like to frequent Constellar from time to time even though they aren't supposed to. Feel free to talk with them only if you are on good terms but don't mention the mission. We want progression not regression. Now if that is all, I think we should get some rest.'

The golden light began to shimmer around their thrones but before they could completely disappear, Brodie jumped up.

'Wait! I need to tell you something from my experience.'

The pair materialised again and gestured for her to continue.

'My counterpart Equas was a truly amazing woman. The poor thing can't stand properly because everything is out of balance right now. She said that someone on Bastion meant to do us all harm and she sensed an uprising. I figured you should know. She wanted you to take notice of her warning.'

Hunter stood up alongside Brodie.

'Come to think of it, I'm pretty sure Ares said that we couldn't be united because there was a traitor but I may not have heard correctly.'

Asterion and Garth exchanged looks. They didn't appear particularly worried.

'Equas is indeed an eloquent and remarkable counterpart,' Asterion agreed. 'It is incredibly unfortunate how much she suffers when our world is out of balance, which didn't happen very often before Milo arrived. However, I wouldn't read too much into her warning. She's been around for centuries and as I'm sure you noticed, is made of stone. The last time I went to visit, she nattered on about an uprising and I told her that is impossible. Bastion is a very calm, peaceful place and we are about to put right the one bad thing that has ever occurred here so please don't focus on what she or Ares the Ram said. Now, let's all get some sleep. You have certainly earned it and tomorrow is when the fun truly begins!'

Chapter 17

Welcome to Bastion

Reilly woke with a start from a horrible nightmare. She had dreamt that her counterpart Chiron and hundreds of other centaurs had surrounded her laughing and pointing whilst she stood in the centre of an amphitheatre gorging on food. She had wanted to stop but the dishes had kept appearing, each more delicious than the next. Chiron had stepped forward and said in the same tone he had that day:

'Is that why Slade chose Danni over you? You eat too much, who would desire that?'

The centaurs had begun to stamp their hooves in a deafening manner whilst Chiron repeated 'who would desire that?' over and over. Reilly had cried and cried until she woke up drenched in sweat.

'Reilly, are you okay?' her best friend whispered in the dark.

Danni had slept in her bed just like old times. It felt so nice to have a sleepover again.

'Yeah,' she whispered back. Even though they had made up, Reilly was clearly not over her insecurities. She wasn't sure how long it would take before Chiron's words no longer hurt and she stopped believing them. She no longer needed a boy to tell her she was pretty, she just wanted to be confident in herself like Parry. Food had always been her comfort in times of need but she hated how it was the first thing she had turned to the night of the Astrological Dance after Slade rejected her. She had binged until the point of being sick. There had to be a different outlet to her pain, a healthier option.

She turned to Danni and noticed she had fallen back asleep. Letting her rest, Reilly went and had a shower. Once she was clean, she changed into purple jeans and a lilac batwing top with cute matching sneakers. She brushed her glossy, dark hair and used her fingers to create more volume at the front. She pictured entering Constellar in a sexy dress and re-doing her experience at the Astrological Dance on a larger scale. Chiron would be standing at the bar, open-mouthed and full of desire for her. She would reject him like a queen and dance all night with her friends. Delicious smells were beginning to waft over from the buffet so Reilly quietly made her way over whilst everybody else slept. She piled her plate full of sweet potato hash browns, grilled mushrooms, tomatoes, cooked spinach and avocado. Garth had clearly tried to recreate meals from back home. She had a soft spot for him after he had cuddled her while she cried. He looked pretty cute in a suit too…

'Reilly?' A male voice behind her made her jump.

She turned to see Slade looking sleepy with tousled hair but still undeniably gorgeous in aqua tracksuit pants and long-sleeved top.

She quickly set her plate down on the counter before it smashed everywhere.

'Slade…umm, what's up?'

The Aquarian shuffled from foot to foot. He was clearly nervous.

'My experience in the Cavern of Aqua helped me realise a few things. I was a jerk to you the night of the dance and afterwards I didn't check up on you when I should've. I didn't apologise for pursuing your best friend right in front of you. I'm a horrible person and I just wanted to say sorry for all the pain I've caused you. I understand if you never want to forgive me.'

Reilly was surprised and grateful. It was completely unexpected but just what she needed in order to heal and move forward.

'Thank you. I really appreciate you saying that and of course I forgive you. I was angry at first but I understand things a lot better now. How are you doing? Does it bother you that Ronan and Danni are getting close?'

Reilly was by nature a blunt and honest Sagittarian. She never meant to hurt anybody with her words, she was just naturally curious.

Slade didn't appear offended.

'I'm okay. I feel really silly. I could tell Danni was hurt from what Crawford did and still I was happy to play rebound guy just to be close to her. I've learnt it's important to be with someone who wants to be with me as much as I want to be with them. I'm sure you understand.'

Reilly nodded. She certainly did. She hoped to sit back from now on and let somebody chase her for once.

She picked up her plate and nibbled on a hash brown.

'How good are these?'

Slade laughed and began piling his plate with food.

'You know, it's weird. We are probably going home tomorrow but I'm going to miss this place. It's been an adventure. How many people can say they've met their astrological counterpart on another planet?'

'Not many that's for sure!'

Reilly walked back to her bed beaming from ear to ear. Her nightmare from earlier was already fading to nothing.

*

After the Astro A Team had eaten lunch, the giant purple doors of the Mission Base were set to open. They were all eager to see what waited outside.

'I bet you anything it looks exactly like *The Fifth Element* out there with flying cars and all!' Drew exclaimed.

'No way, man.' Crawford shook his head. 'Think *Planet of the Apes* minus the apes.'

Drew noticed Charlotte was sulking as usual. Crawford was not giving her as much attention. The spoilt brat was finally getting what she deserved. He was thrilled that his new male best friend was dropping the crazy chick. Double dating would have been super lame. It was weird to think that at one point he would have been double dating with Danni had things worked out. There was definitely chemistry brewing between her and Ronan. He wanted to tease her about going for an incompatible match but figured it was about time she had success in love. Drew, on the other hand, had scored the absolute perfect match. Two water babies swimming side by side, forever and a day…

'Snuggly Bear! The doors are opening!' his white dove squawked.

Sure enough, the gigantic purple doors of mystery began to open up very slowly. Everybody watched with baited breath, unsure of what lay beyond.

A ray of sun blinded their eyes as a typical daytime in Bastion was revealed to them.

Drew had been expecting hovercrafts, robots, lasers and of course aliens. He had envisioned high-rise futuristic towers, lights, sounds and digital marketing for the Bastion version of *Coca Cola*. What he had not been expecting was for everything to look so…normal.

The alternate universe was quiet save for the sound of a nearby bubbling brook. The planet resembled an old town in France with cobblestone paths, dainty brick bridges and fields among fields of wildflowers. Everywhere Drew turned, civilians who looked perfectly normal chattered happily. He was able to identify their sign instantly by their outfit and every now and then he would see an Unsigned wearing a mix of colours. In the distance, he could see the long strip of town that wound through the fields and at the very top stood an enormous observatory made of marble and painted a blue-grey shade.

Overall, Bastion didn't seem particularly exciting nor was it overly big.

'I know what you are thinking.' Garth stepped forward out of nowhere. 'Bastion doesn't look like a big futuristic planet. Don't let appearances deceive you. Beyond Constellar, which is the giant observatory at the top, there is extensive land. There you will find the majority of the Unsigned who feel the homes in town should belong to those who know their sign. I, of course, live with Asterion in the Mission Base. Secondly, Hollywood as you call it, always dramatises everything. We may live on another planet but it operates much the same as yours. The main differences are that this one runs on starlight which powers the town and our species of flora cannot be found on Earth. Enjoy the differences! I was certainly impressed by the thing you call a cactus.'

'Wait, so you have a sun that rises and sets just like back on Earth?' Crawford mused. 'But isn't the town powered by starlight?'

'Yes, starlight powers the town of Bastion much like electricity does back home. That however, is not the sun. It is a planet called Muktu which is also fuelled by starlight. If the counterparts cut off our supply, we will have no "electricity" or "sun".'

'Can everything we need be found in the town?' Parry changed the subject. She looked ready to run.

'Absolutely. Cross the bridge, follow the path and you will enter the town of Bastion. There you will find plenty of stores to get you ready for this evening. In order to reach Constellar, you will need to take a chair-lift that operates next to Wasabi's Tattoo Parlour. Yes, we sell tattoos here and the most common thing to get *is* your sign. You are already covered there…literally.'

Drew shielded his eyes and gazed upward. He noticed wires running from the front of Constellar down into the middle of town. A dainty hand squeezed his. He looked over to see Hannah deathly pale.

'My sweetness, what is wrong?'

'I'm terrified of heights,' Hannah trembled. 'Isn't there another way of getting into Constellar?'

'You could walk but that would take several hours,' said Garth. 'It honestly doesn't take long and the views are breathtaking. You will be fine, my little crab.'

Ronan raised his hand. 'How much time do we have before it opens?'

The afternoon glow from Muktu was warm and bright. By estimation, they had two to three hours before it began to set.

'Constellar opens as soon as Muktu retreats. You will want to get to the chair-lifts a little bit earlier if you can as everybody from town piles into them. I would explore right away, find the perfect outfit and for heaven's sake do your hair!' Garth sniffed in the direction of Hunter.

'Umm, can I ask a really obvious question?' Ambrite squinted, the glare too bright.

'How are you going to pay for everything?' Garth finished.

'Yah!' Ambrite retorted.

'Do you really think the Keeper of the Stars, the Almighty Lord of the Constellations, isn't worth a few shekels? The dude has you covered, okay? Just mention his name and everything will be taken care of.'

'Sweet,' murmured several members of the Astro A Team including Drew.

'Now off you go! Celebrate, drink, and be merry because just for tonight, you will shine like stardust…'

Chapter 18

A Hardened Shell

Hannah needed to distract herself from the upcoming chair-lift that would take her and her friends to Constellar. She decided the best form of distraction was shopping for a dress to wear at the club. Reilly and Danni invited her to walk along the beautiful fields but she declined, wanting time to herself and also to give them space. She kissed Drew goodbye and wandered over the bridge into the town of Bastion. It was so quaint, like the village in Disney's *Beauty and the Beast*. Everywhere she looked, people just like the ones back on Earth were walking to and from the stores. There were teenagers laughing, couples holding hands and children playing in the clean alleys. The only difference between them was they all wore one colour signifying their sign. Hannah noticed an elderly man limping with a cane. He was wearing a brown tweed jacket and tan slacks. She knew none of the zodiac answered to the colour brown which meant he was an Unsigned. Nobody made fun of him but she did notice stares from some of the children and teenagers.

He reached an area with stairs and instinctively Hannah ran over to assist him. Without speaking, she placed his hand on her arm and gestured for him to lean on her. He smiled a wide, toothless grin and pressed his weight against her, taking slow steps. When they reached the top, he nodded in gratitude and patted her cheek. She blushed and waved him goodbye.

Turning back to descend the stairs, Hannah realised a group of people had formed at the base, staring in fascination. She felt incredibly self-conscious as she made her way down. They were still leering as she brushed past them and powerwalked around the corner. Why was it such a big deal that she helped an Unsigned? Were they really so different to the regular citizens of Bastion? Was it so important to know your sign? Back home it hadn't meant anything to her before the Astro A Team had formed.

Relieved the townsfolk weren't following her, Hannah began looking for a store that sold evening dresses. She passed beauty parlours, cafés, bookstores, lingerie stores and even a structure that resembled a post office. On the front, a flashy poster read: *'Write a Letter to your Counterpart!'* Did they actually receive and read the letters? It was evident the counterparts were the celebrities of Bastion. Hannah had the feeling the citizens of Bastion purposely went to Constellar hoping to meet them. Having met Karki, Hannah understood the desire. She missed her crab friend already.

Beyond the post office, Hannah saw an acid green building filled with crazy artwork. The walls were covered in astrological symbols, counterpart caricatures and the four elements. A painted sign in edgy cursive read *Wasabi's Tattoo Parlour*. Hannah could see the chair-lift station next to the shop and gulped. She would deal with that later. A cobblestoned side alley indicated that the fashion district could be found through there. She passed through the alley and emerged into a section boasting colourful clothing stores with the best prices and styles. Her earlier suspicions were confirmed as she observed their use of marketing incentives similar to that of the post office:

Dress to Impress your Counterpart...Win the Favour of your Ruler at Constellar this Evening...Shop at Star-Crossed and you will shine like Starlight.

There were stores selling clothes for all signs and designated stores for just one sign. Hannah couldn't tell which one was best so she entered Star-Crossed purely because it reminded her of her favourite fashion store back home. The entire store was black, filled with pumping club music and had racks upon racks of brightly coloured clothes sorted by sign. The store owner looked a lot like Brodie with perfect white blonde hair and baby blue eyes.

She wore a bright red jumpsuit and crimson lipstick. If her clothes didn't tell Hannah she was an Aries, her energetic mannerisms certainly did.

'Hi!' The owner bounced up and down with enthusiasm. 'Are you here for a dress? Constellar is going to go off tonight and I'm pretty sure the counterparts are going to be there!'

'Umm, yes please,' Hannah answered shyly. 'I really want to stand out for my boyfriend.'

'Oooh,' the girl winked. 'Have I got just the thing! The rack against the back wall is for Cancerians. You will find heaps of dress styles, short- shorts, skirts, jumpsuits and even a full-length, tight bodysuit which looks amazing but you need the goods to show it off.'

Hannah wasn't sure if the girl was insulting her small "goods" but she knew a white bodysuit was out of the question. A lot of the options were scandalously short or busty. Hannah could see they were designed to grab attention. They were the kind of clothes that would horrify any parent. The owner must have witnessed her shocked expression and sashayed over in fire engine heels.

'Problem, sweetie?'

'Ah, do you have anything a little more…conservative?'

The girl raised her eyebrows.

'We do for regular days out in the town but honey if you want your counterpart to notice you, you have gotta dress up! I heard the crab in human form is like a goddess. You two could be best friends but you have to make the effort.'

Hannah felt herself getting angry which was unnatural for her. She usually skipped straight to nervous wreck.

'I'm not interested in making my counterpart notice me. All I care about is my boyfriend and my friends. I can't wear any of this stuff so if you could point out the regular clothes section that would be great…please?'

The girl pouted and pointed to a section near the change-rooms. She turned and bounced over to a pair of girls that had just entered wearing matching sea-foam overalls. Hannah wandered over to the back and instantly found a long white lace skirt with a cotton underlay. She found a thick crop top to match and took them both into the change-room. The outfit looked lovely against her pale skin and red hair. She loved how classy and sexy it was at the same time. Drew would be drooling at her heels. Speaking of heels, she had to find the perfect shoes to complete the outfit. Hannah was about to draw back the curtain when she heard the two Piscean girls giggling and talking nearby. Her heart stopped as she made out the words. It didn't take a rocket scientist to figure out who they were and what they were laughing about.

'The next time he comes to visit us, we should take off our clam bras and see if that doesn't get him in the water!'

'Sirena, you are so bad! He is gorgeous though. I'm sure his dull fishwife won't care.'

Hannah felt her face grow hot. Without thinking, she ripped the curtain open and stood in front of the Piscean counterparts with her clothes in one hand and a balled fist in the other.

'So you are the merskanks that thought you could seduce my man?'

The owner was dancing at the register, unaware of the girl-fight that was about to go down or the counterparts in her store.

The girls had their black and blonde hair tied up in messy buns. One was Asian looking and the other was fair like Charlotte. They stared at Hannah in surprise before realising who she was.

'Ohhh,' the darker one snickered. 'The fishwife has a lot of fire for a cry-baby Cancer.'

'She's just grumpy, Calypsee, because her man hasn't pleased her like he will us.'

The blonde mermaid, Sirena, reached over and snatched Hannah's skirt and top out of her hands.

'Look. She can't even dress to impress. Why don't you stay at home tonight, darling? A real man likes to see more of a woman and we have just the dresses to blow his mind.'

Hannah had to restrain herself from ripping their wavy hair out. A fire was burning inside her like never before. She remembered Drew telling her that the others thought she had no backbone. That memory made the flame burn even brighter.

'Listen here, you sea-bitches,' she spat, snatching her outfit back. 'Drew told me everything about yesterday, how you both cried when he rejected you. That's right, I am more than enough woman for him and trust me, he knows it! If you dare show your faces at Constellar tonight, I will expose you both to the entire club. You can spend the rest of the night being pawed at by every citizen on Bastion. Oh and if you touch him again, I will make sure that Karki snips your mermaid tails off. She may be your friend but she loves me. She will do anything for me and I'll make sure her pincers are put to good use!'

Calypsee and Sirena looked as if they were about to burst into tears which gave Hannah a rush of triumph. The owner, now alerted by the intensity, walked back over.

'Is everything alright, ladies?'

Clearly the citizens of Bastion had never actually seen a counterpart which made them so ravenous for their attention. The owner had no idea she was standing amongst the Piscean Queens.

'Oh, everything is just perfect,' Hannah smirked, handing the clothes over. 'I will take these plus those cute platforms in a size seven near the mirrors. They may not be super revealing but my man likes his women to be classy and leave something to the imagination. Asterion will be accepting the charges for my purchases.'

The girls ran for the door sobbing dramatically. The owner watched them leave. Speechless, she turned and stared at Hannah with a mixture of respect and fear. Hannah waited for her to put the outfit in a carry bag. She accepted the purchases and opened the door. Before Hannah stepped outside, she turned to the owner with a sweet smile.

'Here's a piece of advice…the counterparts aren't as amazing as you think. In fact, some of them are incredibly self-absorbed. Do yourself a favour and dress to impress for you, not anybody else. See you at the club!'

Hannah walked outside, swinging her bag of clothes and humming loudly. Suddenly, the chair-lift didn't seem so scary. She was ready for the night of her life.

Chapter 19

Love Transcending Stars

Muktu was beginning to set and Parry still hadn't picked an outfit for the club. In the past, an event like this would've seen her following a tight schedule. A morning cardio workout, tanning at Maltin's followed by a pedicure, manicure, facial and a wheatgrass shot. She would eat a light breakfast then spend the rest of the morning shopping for an outfit with shoes, jewellery and clutch to match. Finally, her hair and makeup would be done straight after lunch so she had enough time to talk to Graham and plan their grand entrance. Now she was about to go partying at a magical nightclub on an alternate universe and not a single effort had been made. She hadn't even brushed her hair that morning.

What was the point? Being glammed up from head to toe meant nothing if the outcome was dying alone. She hadn't been able to express her emotions to anybody except Hunter when she had accosted him in the showers. Graham had always been her number one confidante but being her male clone, she knew he wouldn't understand. He had also been acting incredibly strange since he had returned from his Coloured Cavern. He wouldn't stop smiling and zoning out.

Parry had an hour to get to the chair-lift. At this stage, she would be going in a jumper, tracksuit pants and zero makeup. She wandered over to a bench near a beautiful, marble fountain and slumped herself down. Closing her eyes, she listened to the calming trickle of the water. It had been all her fault. If she hadn't prioritised looks over everything, she might have had a better relationship with her family. She could've found true love rather than being with somebody just because they looked good standing next to her. Seeing herself ugly and ancient had made her want to throw Perfectionist Parry out and start over. It was exhausting being her. The maintenance was beyond high. The only way she could live with herself now was to become the exact opposite of her old self. The Maiden had wanted her to prove that beauty wasn't everything. She lay flat on her back, staring up at the sky. What could she do to change the outcome of her future and finally feel happy?

She looked up as a group of teenagers dressed to the nines excitedly walked past. Back on Earth, she would've judged their outfits with Graham as if they themselves were without flaw. She shook her head in disgust and lowered her head. A deep longing to be real like Danni, Hannah or even sassy Ambrite ached within her. Suddenly, she knew just how to prepare for the evening. Parry jumped up with a new sense of purpose and strode into a barbershop that read *Hair for Lads.*

A tall, bulky man with a shaved head looked up from his chair with a start. The shop was completely empty. Everyone had probably already left to get in line for the chair-lift.

'Can I help you miss? This is a male barbershop, the female one is in the fashion district.'

Parry noticed a razor on the table. She met his inquisitive gaze with a grin.

'That's okay, I'm exactly where I need to be.'

*

Garth hadn't sugar-coated it, the view was spectacular. As the chair-lift rode ever higher to Constellar, Ronan could see the entire town of Bastion below along with the fields, streams, mountains and far-off landscape that was home to the Unsigned. A magical pink-orange hue hung low in the sky. It made Ronan less homesick for his family knowing that a type of "sun" set in this world the same as it did back on Earth. The chair-lift only took six people at a time for safety reasons so Ronan shared the space with Reilly, Drew, Hannah who didn't seem as scared as he thought she would be, Hunter and Danni. He tried not to stare at her beauty.

She was wearing a yellow ruffle dress that left her shoulders bare. Her brown hair had been curled into ringlets and finished off with a cute yellow bow. Her shoes were simple flats. That's what he loved about Danni. She didn't feel the need to wear tight dresses and lots of makeup; she was effortlessly and naturally beautiful. If Graham's counterpart succeeded in uniting the signs, Ronan wouldn't need to confess his love for her for the sake of the mission. He could do it because he wanted to. The enchanting observatory was the perfect setting. He loved seeing how excited she was, squeezing Reilly's arm and doing a jig as they neared the club.

'Guys, tonight we are going to dance at an astrological nightclub!'

'Dan, you have said that ten times already,' Drew groaned. 'Man, how amazing does my white dove look?'

'Drew you have said that ten times already,' Reilly mocked. 'But yes, she looks incredible.

All the girls did. Hannah looked like a princess in a beautiful white skirt and crop top. Reilly resembled an exotic gypsy in a purple off-the- shoulder dress. A lilac headband fitted nicely amongst her shiny, black locks.

Ronan had picked out a black shirt with skinny jeans and tie. He couldn't help but admire how handsome he looked with his blond hair and blue eyes against the dark shades. Perhaps it had been in his head but when they had met at the chair-lift, Danni had taken one look at him and blushed. He wanted to do the Astrological Dance all over. Instead of seeing Danni heartbroken, he would make her happy in his arms. Drew, Hunter, Crawford and Slade had picked out the exact same clothes as Ronan but in their own sign's shade. The other two boys were in the chair-lift behind them along with Brodie, Ambrite, Charlotte and Graham. Parry was nowhere to be seen. The group figured she wouldn't even show up after her breakdown.

They were only a few minutes away now and Ronan could see Constellar's giant front doors were open with a red carpet leading inside. Scores of different coloured people were waiting in line behind a rope and an enormous, scary bouncer. From the glass walls he could hear a thumping beat which made them all start dancing. Hannah and Drew got a bit too excited and began grinding, Reilly and Danni spun each other around and Hunter, who was still subdued, tapped his feet in time. It was obvious that he and Ambrite were keeping their distance. They had been the two closest friends Ronan had ever seen but somewhere along the way, feelings had intercepted and changed the nature of their relationship. Ronan assumed Hunter had professed his love and Ambrite had naturally declined. His hot-headed friend had a look in his eye that said tonight would be all about drowning his sorrows. In between trying to win Danni over, Ronan promised to check up on him.

The chair-lift finally touched down at the station. The second the glass doors opened, Ronan and his friends burst out and ran to get in line. It wasn't long before the rest of the Astro A Team joined them looking glammed up and excited to enter the club.

'Slade and I were just saying that even LA doesn't have clubs that require a chair-lift to get to. This is the coolest thing ever!' Brodie squealed.

The twins looked incredible in different shades of blue. Slade was rocking his aqua shirt and jeans. Brodie looked stunning in a strapless blue dress with sapphires surrounding the neckline. Ambrite was edgy in neon-green ripped shorts, crop top and combat boots. Charlotte looked pretty in a mustard strapless gown. Graham was decked out in tight burgundy pants and vest and Crawford had pimped himself out in a gold shirt and matching jeans.

'Damn,' Slade whistled, taking everybody in. 'We look fine as hell.'

'We deserve this, team,' Danni smiled. 'We have worked so hard and faced so many challenges. Let's enjoy tonight and hopefully we can go home tomorrow.'

The group whooped in unison. One by one, the bouncer let them through until they stood inside the vast dome of the observatory. Ronan held his breath at the sight before him. The room was divided by an outer, middle and inner circle. The outer circle was a bar that ran around the entire circumference of the club. The bartenders, dressed in skin-tight bodysuits of various colours danced as they took orders and poured alcohol. Glasses upon glasses of vibrant drinks were being whizzed across the bar.

In the centre, a cute punky DJ stood on a raised stage and mixed beats. Ronan saw that she was covered in tattoos and wearing a pair of rainbow overalls. He was surprised that the DJ of Constellar was an Unsigned but everybody that came in shouted and waved at her. She bobbed her head in time with the music, headphones slung around her neck.

The inner circle around the stage was the dancefloor. It was relatively sparse as the club had just opened but the few that had entered were already dancing and drinking. Danni nudged him with her elbow and pointed upwards. Ronan followed her gaze and saw the beautiful glass dome at the top with a gigantic telescope. He imagined taking Danni up to the top, gazing at the stars through the lens and getting close enough to kiss. He scanned the club for an entrance to the roof. By the entrance, another bouncer stood near a velvet rope that barred a spiral staircase winding all the way to the top. Feeling disappointed, he nudged her back and pointed to the stairs. She made a sad face, then shrugged and dragged Reilly off to the dancefloor.

It was amazing being at a club that was so colourful. Girls and boys of all signs moved, kissed, touched and whispered. There were twelve bathrooms for the twelve signs and hidden areas to make out. There were even cages and poles to get up and dance on. Ronan was dizzy and overwhelmed by the lights, sounds and colours. The only thing to do was surrender to it all. He stepped onto the dancefloor and allowed the music to flow through him. A powerful crescendo began to rise and shake the walls. The group minus Parry huddled close and as the beat dropped, they threw themselves into the music. It felt like the last night on Earth as Ronan and his friends danced without a care.

As the strobe-lights flickered on and off, Ronan heard a voice whisper in his ear: 'Have you told her yet?'

The strobe-light turned off and the room returned to normal. Ronan spun around to see who had spoken. He couldn't see anybody but the posh tone suggested his counterpart was wandering around in human form. He took one look at Danni spinning around and made a decision. Abandoning all logic, Ronan strode over to her, took her face in his hands and kissed her. A moment of dread passed through him as he imagined her pulling away or slapping him. Love prevailed however as he felt her fingers running through his hair. She was passionately returning his kisses. He heard Reilly and Drew whooping, which made them smile against each other's mouths.

Ronan was so relieved his legs began to shake from the adrenaline. As they parted breathlessly, he made another decision.

'Danni, I love you...'

A second wave of dread passed through him as he noticed her surprised expression. A moment later, she smiled and took his hand.

'Ronan, I love you too…'

The group broke into applause which caught the attention of the other dancers. The DJ winked at Ronan and put on a slow love song. Danni wrapped her arms around his neck and they began to sway. He was so deliriously happy he couldn't speak. Hannah and Drew slow-danced next to them. The rest of the crowd broke apart and went to get a drink.

'I wasn't sure you felt the same way.' Ronan stared into her shining eyes.

'I do and have for a while,' Danni breathed.

'Even though I'm a Capricorn?'

Danni released her arms, breaking their intimate moment.

'Ronan, I tried dating two guys I'm supposedly compatible with and it fell apart. I'm not going to let the stars dictate who I love. To hell with the stars!'

He laughed at her sudden outburst and pulled her close once more.

'To hell with the stars, you're mine,' he whispered
and knelt down to meet her lips.

Chapter 20

Wasabi

Ambrite had to make a decision. No amount of flashy lights and alcoholic beverages could distract her from needing to think. If the group was sent home tomorrow, she would have to choose whether to join them or not. Immortality sucked. Ambrite had been avoiding Hunter all evening. She was torn between missing him terribly and feeling uncomfortable at the way he looked at her. Things were never going to be the same again and it made her want to howl. Ambrite smiled at Ronan and Danni kissing. They looked so happy and uncomplicated. The group had broken apart to explore. She looked for a place to sit and saw Hunter and Slade heading in her direction. Awkwardly, she ducked and ran into one of the hidden make-out rooms, colliding with a girl reapplying her makeup with a compact mirror.

'Oof!' The girl stumbled. She closed her compact with a snap and spun around angrily.

'See what you did! My lipstick is totally smeared and I'm not allowed into any of the bathrooms to wipe it off.'

Ambrite stared at the beautiful girl before her. Even with smudged lipstick, she resembled perfection. It took a second before Ambrite recognised her as the punky DJ in rainbow-coloured overalls. Her hair was jet black like Ambrite's and shaved at the sides. Her eyes were bright green and almost feline. She had the cutest little freckles dotted around her nose and her entire arms and legs were covered in tattoos of astrological symbols and the elements.

'I'm sorry. I was just hiding from someone,' Ambrite muttered.

Ambrite was about to ask why she wasn't allowed in the bathrooms when it hit her. The rainbow-coloured outfit signified she was an Unsigned which meant she had to do her makeup in a dingy little room with a sleazy couch to get frisky on.

The girl sensed Ambrite's anxiety and softened.

'That's okay, I'm just on break and need to look my best before I go on for another set. I'm Wasabi.'

She extended her hand which Ambrite gracelessly took and shook.

'Ambrite...wait are you the owner of the tattoo parlour next to the chair-lift station?'

'That's me,' Wasabi chuckled. 'Tattoo artist by day, DJ by night. I live in the valley so I have to work harder to make ends meet.'

Ambrite couldn't believe how sensible Wasabi seemed despite appearing the same age as her. She worked two jobs and owned her own place?

'Where is your family? Sorry, that was rude of me.'

Wasabi laughed and sat down on the couch. She patted the seat next to her. Ambrite followed, highly aware that their knees were pressing close together.

'I'm what you would call an orphan. I grew up with adoptive parents who passed away a couple of years ago. I was living in town with them but once they died, I had to leave to make room for another family and was shunned to the valley. By vote of the town, they let me keep my adoptive father's hardware store which I turned into my tattoo parlour. I think they felt sorry for me and offered me a job at Constellar as well.'

Ambrite patted Wasabi's hand and the girl smiled at her with genuine warmth. She remembered the number of people yelling and signalling to Wasabi when they walked in.

'Well, I think you are doing pretty well for an Unsigned. They all seem to love you here.'

'Yeah, I've made a lot of friends. The younger generations don't seem as phased by the Unsigned. It really depends on who your parents are. Some people here think we are pure scum and ignore us. Others treat us normally.'

Ambrite nodded. She could relate, being a lesbian.

'Do the citizens of Bastion make these kinds of decisions then? I thought it was the counterparts that ran Bastion?'

'The counterparts,' Wasabi huffed. 'Who even knows if they exist? Gods know I've never seen them. It's probably just the crazy old man and his lackey living in that cave producing starlight. The elders of Bastion who are less fond of the Unsigned make governmental decisions but apparently they all answer to Asterion who answers to the counterparts.'

Ambrite nearly confessed that the counterparts were real and that her own had even doomed her to eternal life but she stopped herself in time.

'Is it lonely living in the valley?' Ambrite changed the subject.

Wasabi opened her compact mirror again, wiped the smear of lipstick off and started again with a tube of dark purple. The shade brought out the emerald in her eyes.

'Yes and no.' She smacked her lips. 'It sucks being ostracised but I like my own company. After tattooing all day and working the club at night, I like having some time to myself away from it all.'

They sat in silence for a while as Wasabi finished perfecting her look. Once she was done, she turned to Ambrite and gazed into her eyes.

'I've never seen you around before, where did you come from?'

Ambrite felt her face grow hot.

'Ahh, I'm just visiting. I might go back home tomorrow.'

'And where is home?' Wasabi tilted her head.

'Earth.'

Ambrite was surprised to see Wasabi so unmoved by her answer.

'Uh huh, sounds like a nice place. So why aren't you sure if you're leaving tomorrow?'

Ambrite stood up quickly, feeling dizzy. She wobbled as her vision blurred. Wasabi took her hand to steady her.

'You look a bit pale, do you want to go get a drink?'

Ambrite nodded as they walked out together. She noticed Wasabi hadn't let go of her hand. The decision to stay or go had just become a bit easier…

*

The bar was calling his name. Hunter needed a drink and fast. After Ronan had declared his love for Danni on the dancefloor, Hunter and the gang had decided to hit the bar and see what was popular on another planet. Walking towards the counter, Hunter saw Ambrite duck and run into a room with a curtain. It was obvious she was avoiding him and it hurt…badly. For the twentieth time that day, he had mentally slapped himself for being stupid enough to kiss and scare her off. When would she give him the chance to apologise and explain himself? After his meeting with Ares, he had wanted to tell Ambrite how deeply sorry he was for losing his temper. She did not have to feel the same way about him. He just wanted to be close again but that didn't seem possible anymore. No matter how hard he tried to see her as just a friend, he couldn't deny that she looked incredible in her ripped shorts and combat boots. He craved her even more because he couldn't have her. It was sick, messed-up and completely unfair.

'You okay buddy?' Slade clapped him on the shoulder.

'Yeah,' Hunter sighed. 'Let's get a drink, preferably something strong.'

They made their way over to the bar and signalled to the bartender.

'What can I get you guys?' the bartender shouted. He had a shock of orange hair, black sunglasses with a thick frame and a tight red bodysuit that left little to the imagination.

'Ummm…' Slade and Hunter exchanged glances.

'Newbies huh?' The bartender chuckled. Between the red bodysuit and his carrot-coloured hair, he looked ready to burst into flame.

The pair nodded. The bartender stepped back to reveal all of the different brightly coloured liquids on his shelf. They didn't look like the regular spirits you could find back home. These drinks bubbled and popped in their transparent bottles.

'Are they safe to drink?' Slade scratched his head.

'Of course.'

'I'll take the green and purple one.' Hunter was ready to try something new.

Slade ordered a black and red bubbly drink because it resembled his favourite football team's colours.

The drinks were transferred to sturdy glasses and whizzed over to them. Hunter and Slade grabbed their drinks, looked at one another nervously and took a big gulp.

The combination of purple and green turned out to be a flavoursome mix of grape and apple. It was like drinking liquid candy with an alcoholic tang. Hunter downed the entire glass in less than a minute and ordered another one. Slade screwed up his face at the contents in his glass.

'Ugh, it tastes like chilli and tar!'

'Dude, you have to try mine!' Hunter sloshed his glass around. The alcoholic content in just one drink was significantly higher than any he had tried back home.

Slade took a sip and gestured to the bartender for the same spirit in a shot glass.

Hunter wasn't aware how much time had passed between shots and glasses. He remembered Slade stumbling away to be sick. He recalled Ronan checking up on him, his hand in Danni's. At one point, the bartender refused to serve him anymore so he staggered around the room trying to find someone who would. Charlotte and Crawford were arguing in a corner. Hannah was being tickled by Drew. There was a strange man watching Reilly dance and another DJ had taken the stage. He was about to approach another counter when he saw Ambrite and a cute girl who looked a lot like the previous DJ whispering closely and holding hands.

Jealousy ran through his veins as he witnessed an intimacy between them he would never know. The sight made his belly lurch and he ran outside in the cool night air to heave. Groaning, he wiped his mouth on his sleeve and sat back against the wall. The party raged on inside without him. Physically, he felt significantly better but mentally he couldn't stay any longer. He couldn't bear the thought of Ambrite falling in love with somebody else. Hunter stood and approached the station to signal for a chair-lift when he noticed there was already one waiting with a lone figure inside. As the glass doors opened, the girl that stepped out looked exactly like Ambrite. Hunter rubbed his eyes as his vision adjusted to the sight of Parry before him. She was clad in fishnet stockings, a grey denim dress and choker. Her long red locks had been cut into a spiky pixie style and she was wearing smoky makeup around her eyes. She was the spitting image of his unrequited love and that made her even more beautiful than before.

'Wow,' he breathed.

Parry smiled shyly. She bridged the gap between them and tickled his ear with her breath.

'I want to offer you a deal,' she whispered.

Hunter was speechless. He nodded for her to continue.

'Just for tonight, I want you to pretend I'm Ambrite. I want you to do with me what you couldn't do with her...'

The ground swayed beneath him. He must have been dreaming or still heavily intoxicated.

'Okay...and what do you get out of this?'

Parry bit her lip. It was the first time Hunter had seen her truly vulnerable. When she had cried in the showers, he had assumed she was being typical dramatic Parry but there was a new depth in her eyes. She had changed.

'I need you to touch me. I want to be close to somebody for the first time and I don't want it to be with the usual hot, shallow guys that drool after me.'

'Uh, thanks?'

Parry took his hand. In the moonlight, she looked so much like Ambrite. His heart raced. He knew it was wrong but this was an opportunity that wouldn't present itself again. He led her into the chair-lift and they sat in silence as it descended into the sleepy heart of Bastion.

When they reached the Mission Base, it was pitch black and empty. The others wouldn't be back for hours. Hunter couldn't see Parry but he found her lips. If he could pretend she was Ambrite, maybe the pain of seeing her with somebody else would go away...at least for tonight.

Chapter 21

Righting Wrongs

Slade emerged from the aqua-coloured bathroom significantly slimmer. Shot after shot on an empty stomach had been a recipe for disaster.

'How are you feeling, bro?' Brodie grinned. She had been patiently waiting for him outside. Back in the States, they would cover for each other when one of them had partied a little too hard the night before. He was lucky to have a sister who always had his back.

'Yeah,' he groaned. 'It's going to be a hell of a hangover though.'

The music began to thump loudly. Slade covered his ears and winced in pain. Brodie frowned, held up a hand and ran to the bar. She returned moments later holding a glass of what appeared to be water with floating orange orbs in it. Slade took it with a doubtful look.

He took a sip and instantly his headache began to clear. He gulped the rest of the orange-flavoured water and by the last drop he felt back to normal.

'What is this miracle juice?' Slade marvelled at his empty glass.

'I asked the bartender for a hangover remedy and he gave me this. Wow, you look so much better already. If we had these back home everybody would get drunk all the time!'

'Probably a good thing we don't then,' Slade burped.

With his health and energy back on track, Slade gestured for Brodie to follow him as he scoured the club for Hunter who had disappeared. He figured his friend could use some miracle juice of his own. After circling the club three times, Slade figured Hunter had left. It was evident he wasn't handling his situation with Ambrite well. During their search, Brodie had pointed to Ambrite dancing closely to the DJ. Perhaps Hunter had witnessed the same thing and fled. Slade felt sorry for the angry Aries but at the same time, he wanted to shake him and say, 'What did you expect?'

The pair were about to join Reilly, Drew and Hannah on the dancefloor when they simultaneously caught sight of a handsome, tall man staring at Reilly from behind a pillar. From his amethyst eyes to his purple fitted suit, the unshaven stranger was clearly a Sagittarian.

'Why is that guy being such a creep?' Brodie grimaced. 'Does Reilly have any clue she is being stalked?'

Slade looked over at Reilly twirling and spinning to the music. She exuded confidence and independence. He no longer saw the insecure girl living in Danni's shadow. It made him wonder whether he had made a mistake in not pursuing her when he had the chance.

'Hey buddy,' Brodie yelled. Slade snapped out of his trance to run after his sister. She had approached the unamused individual who had broken his gaze from Reilly to flash lilac eyes at her.

'Be gone with you, presumptuous human,' he growled.

'Hey, watch what you say to my sister, man,' Slade jumped in. He placed a protective arm around Brodie who shook it off in annoyance.

'I am not going anywhere! How dare you stare at our friend like some sort of creep? And why do you call us human as if you're not?'

There was an air of majesty to the man that caused Slade to have an epiphany.

'Because he's her counterpart.'

The night before, some of the Astro A Team had shared stories about their experiences in the Coloured Caverns. Reilly had hastily rushed through hers, mentioning that her counterpart Chiron had been a jerk and told her she was undesirable. To make matters worse, he had abandoned her when she began to cry.

Chiron made a hand gesture as if to shoo away a mangy cat.

'You know nothing, children, run along home.'

'Well if you're not her counterpart, I guess you won't mind if we introduce her to you?' Brodie raised her eyebrows.

The siblings grinned as the Sagittarian paled.

'No! Don't tell her I'm here. She despises me after the things I said.'

'I don't get it. Why are you so interested in her after saying such awful things?' Slade sighed. Maybe women were right. Maybe men were the complicated ones.

Chiron looked so miserable, Slade almost felt sorry for him. He may have been the ruler of Sagittarius but his social skills were deplorable.

'I am a proud man and I didn't like that a mere mortal from Earth was trying to change my mind. I can be brutally honest, all Sagittarians are, but my ego took things too far. When she began to cry, I left because I couldn't bear to witness it. I actually find her quite beautiful and very desirable. Counterparts are forbidden to engage romantically with humans so I will adore her from afar. Now leave me be.'

'So you're just going to stand there and stare at her for the rest of the evening?'

Slade chuckled at his sister's horrified face.

Chiron nodded. He crossed his arms defiantly and leant against the pillar.

Slade thought back to his time with Ganymede. His counterpart had confessed to being hopelessly in love with the Maiden but hadn't had the courage to make anything of it.

'Look, you may be forbidden to have a romance with Reilly but she deserves to at least know how you feel. I had the opportunity to be with her and I didn't take it. Maybe I'm the biggest idiot in the world but I still apologised for hurting her. You should do the same.'

The Sagittarian didn't change his stance but his eyes flickered in Slade's direction.

'We are most likely going home tomorrow so now's your chance, buddy.'

Chiron straightened himself, uncrossed his arms and walked away.

Slade exchanged a confused glance with his sister. She shrugged.

'Counterparts…'

*

Brodie watched Chiron disappear into the crowd. He had blatantly ignored Slade's suggestion. Were all the counterparts this frustrating?

'Should we go and tell her?'

'Nah.' Slade shook his head. 'It's our last night here. Let her enjoy it. We can tell her when we get back and it doesn't matter anymore.'

Brodie nodded in agreement. She was proud of her brother for standing up to Chiron. He had clearly grown since joining the Astro A Team. She on the other hand was just beginning to find her voice and was still feeling irritated from last night's discussion with Asterion and Garth. She had told them of Equas's warning and they had dismissed it completely. Brodie was convinced somebody was out to do them harm. Before Chiron had confessed to being in love with Reilly, she had been suspicious of his intentions. She could no longer relax...everybody except her brother was a suspect.

'Hey, guys.' Graham waltzed over. He looked particularly handsome in his tight pants and burgundy vest.

'Hey,' Brodie and Slade replied.

Brodie knew she was being paranoid but something about the Scorpio was off. He had always been an animated guy but the way his eyes kept darting all over the place made her think his drink had been laced with something.

'Have you seen Hunter and Parry?' Graham bounced on his heels.

'No.' Slade shook his head. 'I think Hunter left and Parry never showed. I thought you of all people would know where she was.'

'They need to all be here.' Graham ignored Slade. 'It's important that everybody is here.'

Brodie noticed beads of sweat dripping down his face. He was nervous about something. Without so much as a wave goodbye, he scurried off like a man on a mission.

'What the hell was that about?'

'Who knows,' her brother shrugged. 'I've had the drinks here and they are pretty intense. He probably ordered something that made him a bit loopy.'

Brodie wasn't convinced. Graham had been acting strangely since last night.

'Maybe I should keep an eye on him?' Brodie scanned the crowded dancefloor.

'Relax, Brodes,' Slade groaned. 'You need a hard drink yourself.'

Brodie looked at the inviting dancefloor. Everybody was cutting loose and having a fantastic time. She could've easily joined them and lost herself in the music but her gut-feeling was begging to heed Equas's warning.

'You go have fun, I'm going to follow Graham.'

Chapter 22

The Beginning of the End

Charlotte was a beautiful girl but her negativity and selfishness made her ugly. After Crawford's encounter with Leonis, he had realised just how big a coward he actually was and how scared he was of his "girlfriend". She had tried to make up with him since yesterday but he had kept pushing her away. She wasn't getting the hint but he hadn't exactly told her it was over yet either. What was he afraid of? Being alone? Her murdering him in his sleep? Underneath all of the superficiality, Crawford was worried about how he would look to everybody else.

The entire group disliked her immensely. If they broke up, he would never hear the end of how much of a mistake she was and how they couldn't understand what he liked about her to begin with. If they stayed together however, the group would remain hating her in silence but at least he wouldn't look like a failure. The reality was, whether they returned home tomorrow or not, he couldn't take one more second of being around her.

Earlier that day, she had dragged him off to buy a pair of shoes in town, was rude to the salesperson and slammed the door when they didn't have her size. She had complained that the chair-lift was too dirty. The music too loud. The colours too bright. The people too strange. Enviously he had watched all of his friends dancing and having the time of their life whilst he sat outside the Gemini bathroom holding her purse. He had had enough.

Charlotte emerged from the bathroom reeking of perfume and wearing her trademark unattractive scowl.

'Ugh, those bathrooms are hideous and super cramped. Yellow really is the worst colour, I'm so freaking unlucky.'

Crawford clenched his teeth. He glanced over at Danni looking beautiful with her arms wrapped around Ronan's neck. They were gazing into each other's eyes as if nobody else existed. That could've been him had he not been so stupid and weak-willed. Danni never complained about anything, in fact everything excited her. He loathed himself in that moment.

Charlotte followed his gaze and gave a tinkly superficial laugh.

'Aren't they disgusting? I'm so glad we have the sense to act decent in public.'

Hearing Charlotte refer to them as a couple made his stomach turn. He couldn't take it any longer.

He swivelled to face her. 'We need to talk.'

'Here?' She pouted. 'It's way too loud and plus, I don't want people to think we are fighting.'

She shrieked as Crawford grabbed her by the hand and dragged her into one of the curtained rooms.

'Now listen here,' Crawford fumed, releasing her. 'I am going to talk and you are going to listen. I am not interested in you anymore. I don't want to be with you anymore. Whatever we had, it's over! When we get back home, you will leave me and the group alone. Understand?'

Charlotte could switch moods in the flash of an eye. Now she went from sourpuss to seething in mere seconds.

'What did you say to me?' Her teeth were bared like an angry guard dog's.

Crawford's heart raced and his tough demeanour quickly evaporated. Leonis was right, he really was a coward. Despite being a tiny waif of a girl, she still had the ability to make him shake. He had to stay strong.

'You heard me,' he raised his voice. 'You and I are over! I never should've gotten with you in the first place. The entire group hates you and you're nothing but a whinging brat!'

For one fleeting moment Crawford felt proud of himself but it was instantly turned to shame when Charlotte's lip began to quiver. She burst into tears and stomped out of the room. He shouldn't have added the last part but she had brought out the ugly side in him. He hurried after her to apologise but she had already slammed the bathroom door. Sighing, Crawford sat by the bar and contemplated drowning his sorrows. A bartender with flaming orange hair, black sunglasses and a tight red bodysuit approached him. He wasn't hard to miss!

'I'll have whatever is strongest,' Crawford said, unable to keep the gloom out of his tone.

The bartender removed his glasses. There was something very familiar about his childlike eyes.

'You did well, Crawford, albeit not the most tactful delivery but nevertheless it was brave.'

'Leonis?' Crawford widened his eyes.

The counterpart nodded with an impish grin. He poured Crawford a bright purple drink with flashing orange orbs.

'Drink this.' Leonis handed him the tall glass. 'It will improve your state of mind.'

Crawford took a swig and instantly felt happier. The orange orbs crackling on his tongue reminded him of the candy he loved as a child. The purple portion of the beverage tasted like sweet plums. Maybe he could snag a bottle or two to take home when the time came.

'Why are you bartending here?' Crawford asked. 'Does anybody here know who you are?'

'You cannot confine a Leo, Crawford, surely you know that.' Leonis wiggled his brows. 'I come here because I enjoy being amongst people. My true identity has never been revealed nor will it ever be.'

'I wonder how Asterion feels about that.' Crawford stuck his tongue inside the glass, seeking out any last dregs.

Leonis screwed up his face and poured Crawford another glass but not before taking back the original.

'Asterion does not control what I do. He likes to act the almighty Keeper of the Stars but really he is more of our personal assistant.'

Crawford burst into laughter. Picturing Asterion taking their coffee orders was too much for his already euphorically enhanced state.

Leonis appeared pleased by Crawford's reaction. He poured himself the same drink and took a sip.

'I apologise for calling you a coward, Crawford, it was wrong of me.'

Crawford was still laughing when he noticed the sincerity on his counterpart's face.

'That's okay,' he muttered. 'You were right. I am a massive coward and it took brutal honesty for me to realise it. I haven't had the opportunity to commit a heroic act of bravery yet but I will when the time is right.'

'I know you will. Telling Charlotte the truth was the beginning. When the world begins to fall apart, make sure you are there to do your part.'

Crawford shivered despite the heat of the club. It sounded like advice but he was pretty sure Leonis was making a prophecy.

*

Charlotte sobbed in the vivid yellow bathroom for female Geminis. She didn't know what was more depressing, the colour or her life. It wasn't a surprise that the group hated her but nevertheless it was painful to hear. Crawford had been the one person who had stood by her and even he couldn't stand her now. Brodie, who had offered her friendship in cheerleading class, was also no longer giving her the time of day. Charlotte scanned her entire life starting from childhood to the present moment.

The reality was, she had never been able to keep a loyal, steady friend. She had always been beautiful but her popularity stemmed entirely from her looks and ability to intimidate those around her. Even her own family gave her whatever she wanted so they didn't have to hear her whine. Charlotte had instantly hated Danni. She was the kind of girl Charlotte poisonously envied. Kind, caring, carefree Danni who made friends so easily. Hell, her two best friends had not left her side since kindergarten. That said a lot about the type of person Danni was.

When she had witnessed Danni's ability to form a group at Bouquet Reserve, she had decided to become her arch enemy rather than be positively influenced by her. In the end, she had been able to hurt Danni only through stealing the boy she had loved. The victory however had come with a price. Charlotte had felt instant gratification at Danni's heartbreak but her self-hatred grew stronger in the moments when she was alone and reflected on her selfishness. Even she knew deep down that filming Danni kissing Slade was a low move. Crawford had been a prize to be won but after he had actually expressed interest in her, she had decided to hold onto him. He was after all ridiculously hot and a tool to shove in Danni's face whenever Charlotte's jealousy flared up.

Now, as Charlotte watched her mascara smudge around her face, she felt karma whispering in her ear. Danni and Ronan were blissfully in love and Crawford had officially broken up with her. Charlotte met her miserable gaze in the mirror. Something had to change or she would never have anybody. The best thing she could do for everybody now was to leave when they all returned home and start afresh with new friends. She would try to be more like Danni. She would smile more, listen more and ask others questions about themselves. There would be no life going forward if she continued to push everybody away. Charlotte cleaned herself up in the sink and adjusted her hair. She would begin by finding Brodie and apologising. She emerged from the bathroom only to be nearly bowled over by Graham who was power-walking towards the entrance. She nearly screamed at him but stopped herself. He was acting so strangely.

'Charlotte!' Brodie appeared, out of breath. 'Have you seen Graham?'

Charlotte's face lit up. Here was her chance to make amends.

'I saw him walking really fast towards the entrance. What's going on with him?'

Brodie paused, her hesitation and lack of trust evident on her face.

'Brodie, I know I've been a crappy friend but I'm really sorry. Crawford just dumped me and I want to move on. Can you please forgive me?'

Brodie's eyes widened in surprise. Clearly this was a side of Charlotte nobody had ever seen.

'Ah, yeah of course...water under the bridge. Graham is acting really weird and I just want to make sure he's okay. Come with me?'

Charlotte's heart leapt. Brodie was a classic peace-making Libran who hated conflict. It felt nice to be forgiven and included.

'Let's find him.'

The girls hurried towards the entrance in time to see Graham approaching the bouncer guarding the staircase to the telescope on the roof. He had a wicked grin on his face as he sauntered over and whispered into the man's ear.

Charlotte saw the bouncer's expression change from authoritative to terrified. He nodded and stepped aside. Charlotte couldn't believe what she was seeing. The giant bear of a bouncer was shivering and sweating in fear. What had Graham said to him? Brodie looked at her with the same mixture of confusion and concern. None the wiser, they watched as Graham darted up the stairs to the roof. Brodie and Charlotte marched over to the inconsolable bouncer.

'Excuse me sir, what did our friend say to you?' Brodie shouted over the music.

The bouncer was trembling all over. He was struggling to form words, clearly traumatised. Charlotte felt sorry for him.

'I…can…not…sssay.'

Brodie turned to Charlotte, her beautiful face still so bronzed and glowing.

'Something is clearly wrong. Charlotte, can you please round up the rest of the group and meet me on the roof. I'm going after him.'

The bouncer didn't bother to stop Brodie as she charged after Graham. Charlotte stared after her, unspeakably afraid. The Astro A Team had never considered her part of the group but she now had the chance to do her part. She turned and ran into the crowd. It was time to do the right thing.

Chapter 23

Darkness Falls

With every step he took, Graham climbed ever higher to his destiny. The man he loved, the man he had been waiting for, was waiting for him at the top. They would start a new life together. Nothing and nobody could stop them now. The sweat poured down his face. Graham was running purely on adrenaline. He hadn't been able to find Hunter or Parry but that didn't mean they weren't inside Constellar. He had been given strict orders to round everybody up so Serket's army of scorpions could commit a mass murder. His friends, the citizens of Bastion within Constellar and the Unsigned would be wiped out.

Together, he and Serket would create new life on another planet that would become home to the elite. The night before, Graham had tossed and turned in his sleep. Images of braiding Parry's hair, meeting Danni at Maltin's and being embraced by the Astro A Team on the night he had wanted to leave flashed through his head. They were memories grasping for his attention but none of them had seemed as important as Serket's mission. Yes, the friends he had grown to love would be dead but a life without love was worse than death and he chose that every single time.

Graham finally reached the top, his heart beating rapidly. The moonlight from Muktu illuminated the love of his life. Serket strode towards him, gesturing at the gigantic blue telescope pointing towards the heavens.

'Isn't it pure perfection, my love?' Serket boomed. He was dressed in a long maroon robe complete with hood. His teeth gleamed brightly in the wide open air.

Graham nodded and ran into Serket's outstretched arms. They embraced and all felt right again. Serket stroked his hair and it made him giddy with pleasure. A love like this was worth everything. It was worth what they were about to do.

'Is everybody inside, my darling?' Serket held Graham at arm's length, searching his eyes.

'I was unable to find Parry or Hunter but they were probably in the bathroom at the time.'

'No matter, my babies will find them and finish the job wherever they are.'

'Graham! Move away from him!'

Graham turned to see Brodie standing near the stairs, white as a ghost.

Serket let out an angry growl. Something tugged at Graham again, much like his dreams the night before. He could see his friend was scared but he couldn't understand why that mattered.

'Is this your counterpart?' Brodie slowly walked towards him. 'What does he want with you? What is he going to do to all of us?'

'This is the love of my life, Brodie,' Graham puffed his chest. He was so happy he could finally share the good news. 'His name is Serket and we are going to live on this new planet he made just for us.'

He looked over at Serket expecting to see him pleased but the counterpart was glaring in Brodie's direction.

'What's wrong, my love?' Graham rubbed his arm. Serket brushed him off, leaving Graham hurt and confused.

Brodie shivered. 'Graham, what happens to us when you go to this new planet?'

'Make her go back downstairs with the others,' Serket said through gritted teeth.

Graham was torn with helping Brodie or obeying his man.

'Graham, come back with us. We can talk to Asterion...please,' Brodie pleaded.

'If you do not get rid of her, you will not have my love,' Serket warned.

There was an invisible force inside Graham pulling him in both directions. He kept darting from Brodie to Serket, unable to move.

'Fine.' Serket rolled up his sleeves. 'I will do it myself then!'

Graham watched as Serket waved his hands and laughed as Brodie flew through the air. She hit the floor with a heavy thud.

'Oh!' Graham gasped. He ran over to Brodie who was now unconscious, her forehead dripping with blood. Looking up, he saw Serket smiling without any warmth.

'You disappoint me but I'll just have to remind you where your loyalties lie.'

Graham's eyes widened as he watched a gigantic scorpion tail unfurl from Serket's robes. The stinger was jet black and dripping bright red venom. Serket advanced on Graham who was still kneeling by the unconscious Libran. He was poised to strike when a white light blasted him backwards.

Graham blinked in surprise as Asterion, Garth and the other members of the Astro A Team minus Hunter and Parry appeared on the landing. He watched Charlotte and Slade race over to Brodie and cradle her limp body in their arms.

Asterion and Garth strode over to Serket whose hood had covered his face during the fall. Slowly, he regained composure and shakily stood. As the hood fell, the Keeper of the Stars and his Chief Advisor stepped backwards in shock.

Graham ran over to Serket and threw his arms around his waist. This time, Serket didn't push him away.

'Please don't hurt him! We love each other! Serket and I are going to start a new life together. We will leave right now just don't harm him. Please!'

Asterion looked deeply concerned.

'Graham…that is not Serket.'

Graham stared up at his counterpart in confusion. His head was pounding.

'What are you talking about? You said you have never seen him in his human form so how would you know what he looks like anyway?'

'Because we know who the human is before you,' Garth scowled.

'If that's not his counterpart then who the hell is he?' Slade demanded, fury in his eyes. His sister had not regained consciousness and he wanted revenge.

'Milo.' Asterion and Garth spoke as one.

The group including Charlotte gasped. Graham stepped away from Milo in confusion.

'What? How? No…this cannot be!'

Graham began to feel a sense of normalcy again and the horror at what he had been about to do was starting to pour in.

'What happened to my real counterpart?'

'Dead!' Milo's eyes flashed. 'I drained him of his power when I came to visit and took all his abilities. After I pretended to leave Bastion, I doubled back and resided in the Cavern of Maroon where I plotted my uprising. I had already started a war amongst the other counterparts and was ready to make my move when I found out you brats were coming. It was then I saw my window of opportunity. What better way to hide in plain sight than by seducing a vulnerable boy who needed to be loved and accepted? I stung him with my tail when we met, injecting him with a poison that would make him bend to my will and convinced him to gather all of you here in Constellar. Now if you don't mind, I will be taking Graham and beginning a new life on a faraway planet that is devoid of disgusting Unsigned and those that are not born under Scorpio.'

'What is your problem with the Unsigned?' Ambrite trembled with rage.

Serket regarded her as if she were a tiny ant. 'They are a disgrace to a universe that prides itself on identification through the zodiac. I've already instructed my army to begin with him.'

Graham realised he was pointing straight at Garth who was dancing on the balls of his feet, ready to strike.

Asterion and Garth charged forward along with Graham's friends but it was too late. Milo grabbed Graham's trembling hand and before he could resist, a familiar sting buried itself deep into his palm. The atmosphere around him warped as he fell once more under a heavy layer of seduction.

As the wind blew around the both of them, he heard Milo's imperious voice.

'As we speak, my army of scorpions have infiltrated Constellar and will be destroying all of you one by one. Best of luck. By the morning, I'm sure Bastion will be reduced to nothing but dust!'

Graham gazed up at Milo in adoration. His strong chin, his commanding tone, the depth of his power...he truly was a god among men.

He waved to his friends who were yelling in his direction. Why weren't they happy for him? Milo began to lift him into the air. Graham held tightly to the man he loved. He watched the gleaming red eyes of hundreds of scorpions scurrying across the roof. The deafening sounds of screams filled the night sky. Graham shrugged. Milo was all he cared about now...

STAY TUNED FOR THE THIRD AND FINAL
BOOK IN THE TRILOGY:

'ALIGNING THE SIGNS'

ABOUT THE AUTHOR

Rebecca Rossi

Rebecca Rossi is a 26 year old author who resides in Melbourne, Victoria. Since childhood, she has always possessed an undying love for reading and writing. In 2013, her first novel *Astrology Pond* was published by Serenity Press and in 2016, the sequel, *Facing the Stars* was released. Nothing makes her happier than a cup of tea and a good book. It is authors like Anne Rice and her mentor Eve Old that have inspired & driven her desire to become an author and share her creativity with the world.

Rebecca holds many creative and spiritual passions outside of her work. She is a dedicated vegan activist, registered yoga teacher, blogger and even has her own YouTube channel. In October 2016, she is set to marry the love of her life and is very excited about what the future holds.

If you are interested in learning more, please find her on the following social media channels:

Blog: http://peaceandloveandveggies.com/

YouTube: Peace.Love.Veggies

Instagram: @peace.love.veggies

Tumblr: peaceandloveandveggies